25p

Joan and Lizza Aiken

MORTIMER'S MINE

BBC CHiLDREN'S BOOKS

BR(sc)

JF/c

C706969099

Published by BBC Children's Books
a division of BBC Worldwide Publishing Ltd
Woodlands, 80 Wood Lane, London W12 0TT

First published 1995

ISBN 0 563 40372 1

Typeset by BBC Children's Books
Printed and bound in Great Britain
by Clays Ltd, St Ives plc.

1

On a fine, blowy day in early autumn, not very long ago, a whole lot of things were happening in Rumbury Town, London.

In Rainwater Crescent, Arabel Jones was getting ready to take a walk in the park with her friend Chris Cross and the family raven, Mortimer.

Mrs Jones, Arabel's mother, was about to go and look for a job. And this was because Mr Jones had recently been named Tip-Top Trustworthy Taxi Driver of the Year, with a gold medal and scroll of honour, which had brought him such a lot of extra customers that he was quite worn out, his heart was beating twice as fast as it should, and he had palpitations and high blood-pressure. The doctor had told him to garage his taxi, go to bed, and rest for a month.

As Mrs Jones walked down the path to her front gate, she looked over the fence into the next-door garden where a huge crack had recently appeared. It was beginning to worry the neighbours all up and down the street. It was becoming wider and wider, deeper and deeper. By now it was big enough to hold a double-decker bus.

"*I* don't know, I'm sure," said Mrs Jones, staring at the hole, which today had nearly reached the fence. "I've written to the Council, I've phoned; I can see I shall have to go round there and give them a piece of my mind."

"But Ma," said Arabel, standing on the doorstep to say goodbye, "Mortimer *likes* the hole. He puts things in it."

Indeed, just at that moment Mortimer the raven, sitting on the fence, threw an old toothbrush of Mr Jones's down into the pit. And he followed this with a pair of holey socks.

"Just don't let him put anything else in!" said Mrs Jones, rather upset. "I don't want future generations to find my ironing in there. Somebody ought to make Mr Leggit pay to have it filled up."

Mr Leggit was the owner of the garden next door. But he was away in jail, for stealing computer tapes from the Town Hall.

Upstairs, in his bedroom, Mr Jones sat gloomily by the window, testing his blood-pressure on a Test-Your-Own-Blood-Pressure kit that Mrs Jones had kindly bought him. Each time he looked out of his window at the huge hole, the pointer on the machine's dial shot up by six points.

A couple of miles away, in Rumbury Jail, Mr Leggit was grumbling at his pigeon. This bird had been given to him under a *Pets for Prisoners* scheme. Its name, on a label round its leg, was Pio Nono. It lived in a box on his cell window-sill. Unlike Mr Leggit, the pigeon could fly away whenever it wanted. He was trying to train it to take messages to his assistants, Bill and Joe, the Cash-and-Carry Boys.

Mr Leggit was also planning a sticky end for Mortimer the raven – if only the pigeon would listen to him and pay proper attention.

In the Town Hall, Bill and Joe, who used to work for Mr Leggit robbing banks and TV shops, were turning over a new leaf. Instead of having been sent to prison, they were doing five hundred hours of useful community work for Rumbury Council.

Or that was the plan. Mr Cutlink, the new Mayor, was telling them what to do.

And far away from London, on the island of Pollyargos, the people who lived there were packing up a huge parcel to send to Rumbury Town. Last year, after the island had been devastated by an earthquake, the Rumbury ladies had knitted them a great many scarves, cardigans, mittens, and tea-cosies. And this parcel was the Pollyargans' way of saying thank you.

"Goodbye, Ben dear!" Mrs Jones shouted up at the

bedroom window, where she could see her husband's mournful face behind the glass. "Now, remember what the doctor said – if you get restless, take a nice warm bath."

"I can't," Mr Jones said glumly. "The bath drain's blocked."

"I've got a friend who's a plumber," said Chris Cross, who came whistling along the pavement just at this moment. "She's called Have-a-Go Flo. She works for the Council. Shall I give her a call and ask her to come round?"

"Oh, thank you, Chris dear. You're a paragon. Now, you be good, you two," Mrs Jones said to Arabel and Mortimer. And she hurried off in search of a job.

Mortimer rushed to Chris, and began searching in his pockets.

"All right, all right, Mortimer," said Chris. "Here you are, I've brought your Mortimer bar."

"Kaaark!" said Mortimer.

The Mortimer bar was a new invention. It was made with layers of chocolate, peanuts, raisins, marzipan, biscuit, and butterscotch, covered in chocolate, and wrapped in red-and-gold paper. Just at present, these bars were Mortimer's favourite food. For just a moment, holding it in his beak, Mortimer did think about dropping it down

the deep hole in Mr Leggit's garden. But in
the end he decided to swallow it, paper and all.

"*Nevermore . . .*" he said, then hopefully looking to
see if Chris had brought another.

But Chris had not brought another. "Sorry,
Mortimer," he said. "That's your lot. Come on, let's
go to the park."

So Chris and Arabel set off along Rainwater
Crescent, pulling Mortimer behind them on his
trolley.

In the Town Hall the new Mayor, Mr Cutlink, was
talking to Bill and Joe.

"Now, boys, ahem! There's a little preventive
device connected to those anklets you are wearing,
just to keep you on the straight and narrow. A stitch
in time keeps the doctor away. If, by chance, you
should happen to stray outside Rumbury Borough,
an alarm bleep will go off which can be heard all over
the Northern Hemisphere. I'll demonstrate." An
ear-shattering howl began. "And if I press this button
twice—" Mr Cutlink demonstrated again, "– that
means you are wanted back in the office."

"Blimey!" said Bill. "Sounds like someone pinched
the Tower of London."

"Right?" said the Mayor, switching off again.
"Now, first I'd like you to stick up these posters

advertising the Rumbury Town Pop Festival. There are six hundred of them. Put them on walls, trees, fences. Then, when you've done that, come back here and pick up some books that have been discarded from the public library. And I'll tell you what to do with them."

"Murder!" muttered Joe. "This is worse than my mum."

There was a knock, and the door opened. Mr Barnoff, once a policeman, now the Mayor's personal assistant, came into the room leading a large shaggy dog.

"What's *that*?" demanded the Mayor, staring at the dog with disfavour.

"He's on loan, sir, free, from the hospital. A Personnel Calming Device. P. C. Dog, they call him. Council staff are supposed to pat him at regular intervals to keep tension at a low level."

"Well, *I* don't want him," fretted the Mayor. "There's nothing wrong with *my* tension. Sleeping dogs gather no moss."

"He's a gesture of goodwill, sir."

The dog curled up and went to sleep on a pile of computer print-outs.

Bill and Joe looked at one another, raised their eyebrows wearily, picked up an enormous roll of posters apiece and went off to stick these on the first vertical surface they could find.

At Number Six, Rainwater Crescent, Chris's friend the plumber had arrived. She had red hair, wore a boiler suit, and carried a huge bag of tools. She strode vigorously up the front path and stood with her elbow pressed on the door-bell button, while she stared disapprovingly at the huge hole in Mr Leggit's garden next door.

When at last Mr Jones, wearing pyjamas and looking put-out, opened the door, she said, "Are you Mr Jones? I'm the plumber, Have-a-Go Flo. Drains fixed, leaks plugged. That's a very nasty crack you've got there next door. I'd be worried about it, if I was you."

"I *am* worried," said Mr Jones crossly. "And our bath-pipe's blocked. And our washing-machine's out of order."

"Isn't your neighbour doing something about that hole?"

"Leggit? He can't, he's in prison."

"Oooh! Is it him what burgled the Town Hall and got pinched by a raven?"

"It was our raven," said Mr Jones. "Look: I'm not well, I've got to go back to bed."

"Okay, I'll get on with the job then," said Have-a-Go Flo, cheerfully. "Just let me have a look at your deep seal trap."

"Deep Seal Trap?" muttered Mr Jones. "What's

that? This isn't the Antarctic. Though it feels like it."

Shivering, he went back to bed.

In Rumbury Jail, Mr Leggit had just been given his lunch through a hatch in the cell door. The lunch was a jam sandwich, very dry and curled-up. Mr Leggit peered at it disgustedly. But Pio Nono came hopping in between the bars of the window, his pink eyes bright with hope.

"Coooo!" said the pigeon.

"No – you don't!" snapped Leggit, whipping a corner of his blanket over the tin sandwich-plate. "You'll get yours when you've done some work. Come on, now! What do you do?"

He pointed to a drawing of Mortimer the raven on his cell wall, and chanted in a loud snarling voice: "*Bring* me back the *Raven*! *Bring* me back the *Raven*!"

Pio Nono wore a whistle on a wire frame round his neck. After listening glumly to Mr Leggit for ten minutes or so, he at last got the idea, and repeated the phrase on his whistle: "*Too*tle tootle *too*, too! *Too*tle tootle *too*, too!"

"About time too!" said Leggit.

The prisoners on either side thought so as well. They were banging indignantly on their cell walls.

Mr Leggit gave the pigeon half his sandwich, remarking, "Personally, I'd sooner eat the plate."

Meanwhile Arabel, Mortimer, and Chris were coming back from the park, walking across Rumbury Waste. This was a large empty stretch of land alongside a tower block on legs. The block was called Rumbury Tower Heights. The land could not be built on, for it often flooded. The tower block, which had been put up by the Council, was standing empty at present.

Chris Cross was carrying two rolls of bus tickets, fourteen conkers, a plastic spade, a soda can, and a pink glove. Now Mortimer offered him half a brick which he had found lying under Rumbury Tower Heights, among its legs.

"Look here, Mortimer," said Chris, "my pockets are full up. I can't carry anything else."

"He's collecting things to put down his mine," explained Arabel. "The hole in Mr Leggit's garden, you know. Ma has told him not to put in things from the house."

"Next time we'll bring a garbage sack," said Chris, pausing to read one of the posters which Bill and Joe had stuck all over the legs of the tower block. "Hey, Arabel, look at this! SING A SONG FOR RUM-BURY! it says. 'Apply to the Mayor if you want to take part in the Rumbury Open Air Pop Festival!'"

"Ooh!" said Arabel. "*You* could do that, Chris. You make up lovely songs."

"Rumbury, Rumburee!" sang Chris. *"It doesn't have mountains, doesn't have sea, but my friends live here, as you can see, that's why I stay in Rumburee."*

As he sang this, up above, over their heads in the tower block, Chris and Arabel heard a flittering and a fluttering.

"Hush! Chris," said Arabel, pointing to another sign, stuck on a post beside the big building. "Look what it says here. RARE BATS LIVE UP ABOVE. DO NOT DISTURB THEM."

Mortimer, now seeing this signpost, came hurrying over and tried to dig it out of the ground with his beak.

"No, you mustn't take that sign, Mortimer," said Arabel. "It's for the bats."

"Kaaark!" said Mortimer disgustedly.

"I'll make you one for yourself, if you want," Chris told him. "We could put up a post in your garden, with a notice on it that says MORTIMER'S MINE. TIP YOUR UNWANTED ARTICLES HERE."

Mortimer, charmed by this idea, at once began hurrying towards home. Chris and Arabel put the half-brick on the trolley, and followed.

Up at Rumbury Town Hall, the Mayor had opened a letter out of the huge pile awaiting his attention, and cried out in excitement: "Hey! Barnoff! Listen to this! Some outfit called Bonnybuy's Supermarkets wishes to open a new Superstore in Rumbury! Many a true word lays golden eggs!"

Barnoff said, "Bonnybuy? Is that the Texas tycoon? I read about him in the paper. He wanted to buy Windsor Castle."

"Fancy!" said the Mayor. "Now – I wonder if we could get him interested in Rumbury Tower Heights? Barnoff, we badly need money. The town account has been overdrawn for five years. If we could sell him the Heights—"

"Foreigners mostly seem to go for old phone boxes, sir," pointed out Barnoff, discouragingly.

"*Do* they?" said the Mayor, amazed. "I wonder why? Maybe we could throw in a couple of old phone boxes with the Heights. There are plenty of dud ones about the town. But, Barnoff, there's another thing – we've got to do something about that hole in Rainwater Crescent. I've had dozens of complaints. That's going to cost a fortune to fill in."

"You could send a bill to Leggit," suggested Barnoff.

"In jail?" The Mayor thought about it. "Barnoff, that's not a bad idea. Spilt milk is better than no bread."

In Rainwater Crescent, Bill and Joe were looking for a place to stick up their last three hundred posters. They passed by Leggit's front garden.

"Dearo, dearo, just look at that hole," said Joe, peering over the fence. "How about chucking the rest of the posters in there, eh?"

"Maybe the Mayor's bleeper would go off," said Bill doubtfully. "Say, that hole does look a bit dwinjey, don't it? Think we should send Leggy a card about it?"

"Nah. Not the kind of news he'd want to hear," said Joe.

Have-a-Go Flo came whistling along the pavement and stopped.

"Disgraceful, that hole – needs filling in, don't it?" she said. "You two from the Council?"

"You could say that," said Bill, carefully.

"Ought to be seen to," said Flo, striding up the Jones front path. She shouted up to the window above, "Yoo-hoo, Mr J! I've brought your new washer!" – balancing her bag of tools on the fence.

Chris, Arabel, and Mortimer came through the gate behind Flo.

"Hey – Flo!" called Chris. "No need to bring Mr Jones down again. We've got a front-door key."

Mortimer the raven now shot past Flo and slammed in through his raven-flap with a loud crash.

Flo was so startled that she let go of her tool-bag, which hurtled down into the chasm in Mr Leggit's front garden.

2

Next morning, as Mr Leggit drank his breakfast tea in jail, he was surprised by a heavy packet falling with a thump on his floor, and a voice through the hatch: "Special delivery, Prisoner Leggit."

When Leggit opened the packet, he found it to be an enormous bill, fifteen metres long. As he unrolled it, the long strip of paper completely covered the floor of his cell.

"I don't believe it!" he gasped, staring at the rows of noughts.

"Coo," said the pigeon, staring over his shoulder.

"It's all right for *you*," growled Leggit. "You don't have to pay it. How am I supposed to get this kind of money, locked up in here? I can't rob a bank. And what the blazes has been going on in my front garden?"

"Who?" said the pigeon.

"It's not *who*, it's *why*? If you'd stop asking stupid questions, I could work out how to get a message to the boys."

Disappointed, finding that the bill was not something to eat, the pigeon hopped out through the window-bars. But Leggit, suddenly struck with a bright idea, grabbed its tail and yanked out a feather.

"Ooooo!" said the pigeon.

"You've got plenty, you'll never miss it," said Leggit, dipping the pointed end of the feather in his tea and beginning to write on a handkerchief. "I just hope the boys haven't forgotten how to read . . ."

In the kitchen of Number Six, Rainwater Crescent, Mr Jones was pottering about. He was feeling a little better today. This was because his Test-Your-Own-Blood-Pressure machine had gone wrong. The needle on the dial stayed at zero all the time, instead of swishing round and round. So Mr Jones had got up and was making bread. He had a huge pan of dough rising up like a football. It smelt warm and yeasty and delicious. He had set the kitchen timer to tell him when the dough should be put in the oven to bake.

Outside the front door Have-a-Go Flo the plumber was fishing for her tool-bag down the deep hole in Mr Leggit's garden. She had twenty metres of rope and a long-handled pruning-hook.

Mortimer the raven was trying to help.

"I think perhaps you'd better come inside the house, Mortimer," said Arabel.

Mortimer came reluctantly. And, once he was in the kitchen, he wanted to sit in Mr Jones's dough. He thought it was a cushion. Arabel had to take him into the lounge and try to distract him by playing Hunt-the-Slipper.

"*Got it!*" shouted Have-a-Go Flo at last, triumphantly. She hoisted up her bag of tools and brought it into the house. "Now I can finish clearing your bath drain, Mr Jones."

"And don't forget the washing-machine," mentioned Mr Jones, testing his blood-pressure for the eighteenth time that morning.

"Looks as if that thing's on the blink, too," said Have-a-Go Flo peering over his shoulder. "Want me to fix it? See, the ratchet has slipped."

As she adjusted the ratchet, Mortimer came in from the front room and jumped on to the pump of the blood-pressure-testing machine. At once the needle began whizzing round and round the dial. Mr Jones let out a yell of alarm, just as the kitchen timer went off. Mortimer, startled, fell backwards heavily into Mr Jones's pan of dough.

At this moment, Chris Cross popped his head round the back door.

"Hello, everybody!" he said. "It was so quiet in here, I thought you must all be out."

"I give up!" said Mr Jones, heavily. "I'm going back to bed."

"I'll take Arabel out to the park," said Chris. "It's a good day to practise songs for the competition."

"And I'll just see to the bath drain," said Flo. "I've fixed your washing-machine, Mr Jones."

"What about Mortimer?" said Mr Jones. Mortimer was still lying luxuriously in the dough, in a raven-shaped hollow, with his feet in the air.

"I put your sign up in the garden, Mortimer," said Chris. "It says MORTIMER'S MINE." Mortimer tore himself joyfully out of the dough, and crashed out through his raven-flap.

"Thanks, Chris," sighed Mr Jones, and taking his blood-pressure kit he crept back upstairs.

Mortimer was so delighted with the sign saying MORTIMER'S MINE which Chris had nailed to the garden fence, that he could not be persuaded to come for a walk in the park. So Arabel and Chris went off without him. As they left, they passed Bill and Joe, coming slowly and wearily in the opposite direction, wheeling a large trolley full of books which had been withdrawn from Rumbury Borough Library.

"This community service is going to be the death of me," said Bill.

"Hey, look, Bill," said Joe. "That bird's waving at us."

"Not that plumber dame? That Have-a-Go Flo?" said Bill nervously. "If we don't watch it, she'll have us filling up that hole in Leggy's garden."

21

"No, no, not her. That flea-bitten pigeon there, on the fence."

As he said these words, Pio Nono flew over the boys and dropped a grubby handkerchief on Bill's head. Joe nearly fell over laughing.

"It's a dove! It's a message of peace!" he said.

"Hang on," mumbled Bill, staring at the handkerchief, "I think it *is* a message. It says here: 'Get dough for hole. And snatch rook. Tony.' What can that mean?"

"Tony? Toe – knee! It's from Leggy! A message from our pal in prison!"

"But what does it mean?"

At that moment Mortimer, who had been down in the bottom of the deep hole in Leggit's garden, came scrambling up over the edge and said, "Kaaark!"

Disconcerted, the boys looked at Mortimer, looked at the hole, looked at each other.

"Ah," said Joe. "Two birds with one stone. What does it mean? It means 'Get dough for hole. And snatch rook.'"

Over at Rumbury Town Hall, the Mayor and his assistant Barnoff were opening two large boxes which had been sent round from Rumbury Technical College.

"What's this?" muttered the Mayor, examining a

22

large metal prong like an egg-beater with a sponge attached to the end.

"It's a pair of robots, sir, it says here. A contribution from the college for your *Clean up Rumbury* programme."

"Humph," said the Mayor. "Robots? That's not a bad notion. Supposing they work, that is. We shan't have to pay them. Work without pay builds Rome in a day."

"And here's a fax, sir, from the inhabitants of Pollyargos. *We ghaf you large ghift to thanks for aid.*"

"Now that *is* heart-warming," said the Mayor. "I'm very much touched. The Pollyargans send us a gift in return for our knitting. – But where is the gift?"

"Perhaps it will come by the second post."

"I wonder what it can be? Did you say *large* gift?"

"A dolphin, do you think? A dinosaur? A donkey?" said Barnoff, absently patting the Council Dog.

"Where in the world are we going to keep it?" fretted the Mayor. "If it's big?"

"On Rumbury Waste?"

"No good, Barnoff. Remember, the Pop Festival is to be held on Rumbury Waste."

"But what about the bats in the tower block?" said Barnoff. "If those bats are upset by the music, we'll have the environment people down on us like a ton of bricks. Bats have very keen ears."

"Hear today, gone tomorrow," said the Mayor.

There was a knock at the door. The Town Dog barked. In came Chris and Arabel.

"Is this where they have auditions for the Festival?" asked Chris. "We've got a song about Mortimer. We want to sing!"

In Rainwater Crescent, Bill and Joe were throwing armloads of books into the huge hole in Leggit's garden. As they worked they sang:

"He's black and I'm white

When we've had a wash on Friday night

He's fat and I'm thin

We're working down the mine

And we're filling it *in*!"

"Hallo, very nice, boys," said Mrs Jones approvingly as she walked up the path to her house and opened the door. "Yoo-hoo, Ben? Ben? I'm home!"

"I'm in the kitchen, Martha," called Mr Jones. "I'll bring you a cup of tea in the lounge."

Feeling a bit better after a nap, Mr Jones had crawled downstairs and mixed up a new lot of dough.

"Ooh, Ben, that's lovely," said Martha, flopping into an armchair and sipping her cup of hot tea.

"*Such* a day I've had. Could I get a job? No I could *not*. No school helpers will be requited, they say."

"You mean helpers don't get paid?"

"So they said."

"Well, *that's* no use," said Mr Jones. "Oh, Martha, will you have a look at my dough, see if it's ready to bake?"

"I thought it was ready this morning?" said Mrs Jones, puzzled.

"That lot got full of feathers. I had to chuck it in the bin."

But when Mrs Jones went into the kitchen, the dough pan was empty. Mortimer had hoisted the big floppy lump of unbaked bread out through his raven-flap and dropped it into the hole, where it fell on the heads of Bill and Joe, and the discarded library books.

3

Next day Mrs Jones said, "Ben, I'm off to the Town Hall today. Maybe *they* can find me some kind of job."

"While you're there," said her husband, "you might remind them about that hole in Leggit's garden."

"I'll *remind* them," said Mrs Jones. "But with that lot, it's in one ear and out the other."

Chris and Arabel were going off to the park to practise their song. They took Mortimer with them, perched on Chris's guitar case.

Mortimer was not at all pleased at being taken. He would have preferred to stay by his new signpost and toss empty milk bottles into his mine. But the supply of milk bottles in Rainwater Crescent had run out. So he rode on the guitar case muttering in a dissatisfied manner and looking peevishly from side to side.

Up at the Town Hall, Mrs Jones found the Mayor full of enthusiasm for his new robots. Guided by a remote control, they were learning to sweep the floor, put papers into cupboards, make tea, and clean the windows.

Or that was the plan.

One of them also tried to sweep the Council Dog, who growled and removed himself.

"Here's a hundredweight of acorns for you, sir," said Barnoff, coming in with a heavy sack.

"I'm sure I never sent for them?" said the Mayor.

"Yes, you did, sir. The schoolchildren are going to plant oak trees on Rumbury Waste."

"Oh. Well, we must get the Pop Festival over first," said the Mayor. "Never offer your hen for sale on a rainy day. When is that American supermarket fellow coming to see me? I'd like to show him the Tower Heights before Rumbury Waste is covered all over with Coke cans and gum wrappers."

"Mr Bonnybuy is coming tomorrow, sir. I've sent the lads to find him a couple of phone boxes."

"*Phone boxes?* Whatever for?"

"To sweeten him up, sir. And here's a letter for you."

"A letter? Looks like Greek to me."

"It *is* Greek," said Barnoff.

Meanwhile, beside Rumbury Tower Heights (which was beside the children's playground), Bill and Joe were staring at a couple of ancient, cumbersome heavy red phone boxes.

27

Bill said: "Old Barny told us to fetch them up to the Town Hall. But how? Just tell me *how*?"

Joe, looking over Bill's shoulder, said, "Hey. D'you see what I see?"

Bill turned to look. Have-a-Go Flo was striding across the thistly grass towards them, swinging her tool-bag as if it was filled with feathers, not tools.

"Hi, guys!" she said. "What's new?"

"Hi, Flo!" said Joe. "We've been told to shift these phone boxes up to the Town Hall. Fancy having a go?"

Flo turned and gave the boxes a measuring look.

"Just let me get at 'em," she said.

Soon Bill and Joe, assisted by Have-a-Go Flo, had hoisted the two derelict phone boxes on to a trolley. Bill and Joe started wheeling the trolley along Rainwater Crescent, towards the Town Hall.

In Rumbury Park Arabel and Chris were practising their song, while Mortimer was having trouble with a pigeon. It kept following him about, teasing him by playing a little tune on a whistle which hung round its neck on a frame.

Becoming very bad-tempered, Mortimer reached forward, swallowed the pigeon's whistle and gave it a box on the ear.

"Oooo!" wailed the pigeon, falling backwards into a litter bin.

"Hic!" said Mortimer. "Kkaaaaa – wheee – hic!"

"Oh, dear. Have you swallowed something, Mortimer?" said Arabel, turning round.

"There's never been a time when Mortimer hasn't swallowed something," said Chris.

"Hic – wheee!"

"Hey – look!" said Chris. A beautiful girl was coming towards Arabel and Chris across the grass.

"Try holding your breath, Mortimer," Arabel advised.

"Or standing on your head," Chris suggested.

"My goodness me, what a beautiful creature!" exclaimed the girl, coming closer. She had jet black hair, just the colour of Mortimer's feathers, done in a long plait down her back, lots of bangles and neck- laces and beads, and she wore a shimmering sari. "What kind of a bird is he?" she asked.

"He's our raven, Mortimer," said Arabel. "And he's got hiccups."

"Perhaps I can help?" said the girl. "So!"

She leaned over Mortimer, taking him completely by surprise, and clamped his beak tight shut with one hand. She waved the other hand slowly up and down before his eyes.

"Oh, *do* take care!" gasped Arabel anxiously.

"*Now!*" said the girl to Mortimer. "*Sing!*" And she let go of his beak.

Hugely astonished, he gave out a long, melodious *kaaark!*

"See?" said the girl, laughing. "No heecups! Singing cures all." Mortimer gazed at her, quite stunned and bewitched.

"Are you in the music business too?" asked Chris.

"Why, yes," said the girl. "I am Seleena the singer. Far away in India I am very famous with my group, the Sand Boys. Now I am here to improve my English."

Arabel said, "There's going to be a song contest here in Rumbury. Are you going to be in it?"

"This I would like very much," said Seleena.

"Come home with us and have some tea," said Arabel. "Then we'll take you to see the Mayor."

Up at the Town Hall, Mrs Jones and the Mayor were at cross purposes.

"Some people," said Mrs Jones, "think cleaning is demeaning. But myself, I see it as an art form. Now this office of yours, Mr Cutlink, could do with a good rub."

"That's why we have robots, my dear Mrs Jones," said the Mayor, as a robot trundled in carrying two slopped cups of tea in a dustpan. "The robots do the rubbing, ha, ha! A blind horse is better than a nod from a lord."

"Oh, I see. You're on automatic, are you?" said Mrs Jones, disappointed, as the robot slapped the tea on to the Mayor's desk. "I was going to offer *my* services."

"I'm sure your home is quite irreproachable, Mrs Jones," said the Mayor politely. "In fact, I was just about to ask you if you and your family would take in a special guest."

"A *guest*? When we've a hole next door you could put dinosaurs in and never know you'd lost them?"

"*This* guest, Mrs Jones, is Professor Tigran, from Pollyargos. He wishes to study the habits of a typical British nuclear family while he is here supervising the instalment of the Gift from his grateful fellow Pollyargans. And – ahem – I thought at once of you and Mr Jones and your charming daughter and – er – house-pet—"

"Well – I dunno," said Mrs Jones, somewhat softened. "I'd have to see what Ben says—"

"Of course, the Borough would be pleased to pay for Professor Tigran's board and lodging."

"Oh, well – in that case – But we're *not* a nucular family, Mr Cutlamb. I don't hold with those nucular devices, not at *all*—"

Chris, Arabel, and Mortimer had come back from the park and gone into Number Six for tea. But

Mortimer stayed outside and was sitting on his sign-post, wishing for more socks, half-bricks, bus tickets, and milk bottles to throw down his mine.

When he saw the boys coming along the street, wheeling a trolley with two phone boxes on it, his eyes began to sparkle. He sidled along the garden fence and round the corner until he was sitting on Mr Leggit's front gate. Then, as the boys came alongside, he suddenly leaned forward and shouted, "NEVERMORE!"

"Yikes!" gasped Joe, swerving and tripping. "It's the Talking Eagle!"

The front phone box lurched and toppled against Mr Leggit's fence, so that it was hanging over the edge of the huge hole. The fence began to snap, all along. Then fence and phone box shot down into the chasm.

Mortimer let out a loud squawk of joy.

Mr Jones opened his bedroom window, leaned out, and bawled, "What's going *on* down there?"

"Oh, it was just your bird, Mr Jones," sighed Joe. "Knocking something down."

Arabel, Chris, and Seleena came out of the Jones front door.

"Is that you, Pa?" Arabel called up to the window. "I thought you were asleep. I wasn't going to disturb you."

"I *was* asleep," said Mr Jones bitterly.

"I just left you a note. We are going up to the Town Hall with Seleena. This is Seleena, Pa. But we shan't be long."

Arabel, Chris, and Seleena went off up the road, Arabel carrying Mortimer.

Mr Leggit's pigeon flew down and landed on the boys' trolley, beside the second phone box. It had a black eye and a torn collar.

"Is that Leggy's bird? What's happened to him?" said Bill. "D'you think we ought to bandage him up?"

"What about this other phone box then? They won't want just *one*?"

"Down the hatch, why not? It'll be doing Leggy a favour, filling up his hole."

They tipped the second box after the first.

"Hullo, boys," said Mrs Jones coming along the street. "Working hard, are you? That's the ticket!"

She went into the Jones house, calling excitedly, "Ben, Ben! Just listen to this!"

Mr Jones trailed slowly downstairs. "Yes? What?"

"Ben, there's an Ancient Greek Doctor coming to Rumbury, and the Mayor's asked us to put him up for the ceremonials in our residence. Because we're a Focal Family!"

"That's all I need!" said Mr Jones.

Chris and Arabel had taken Seleena to the Town
Hall. Just now, the Mayor's office was quite crowded
with the Council Dog, two robots who were
polishing the legs of Mr Cutlink's desk, Arabel, Chris,
Seleena, Mortimer, and the Mayor himself.

"This is Seleena. She would like to sing in your
contest, Mr Cutlink," Arabel said. "In India she is a
famous film star."

"That's splendid, splendid!" said the Mayor,
politely. "For Miss Seleena we can forget the entry
formalities – just you sing us a nice song for
Rumbury, my dear! Sing before breakfast, you know,
laugh after tea."

"Yes, yes!" said Seleena. "I think it shall be a
happy song – already it is coming to me." She stood
still, rapt, taking a deep breath.

Mortimer, perched on the Mayor's desk, gazed at
her devotedly. Ever since she had cured his hiccups
he had a deep respect for Seleena.

"When you get that golden feeling..." Seleena
sang. "Then your heart flies through the ceiling –
And I've got that golden feeling – NOW!"

On the word *now* Seleena hit a tremendously high
top note. All the light bulbs swung about, several of
the windows cracked, Mortimer fell over backwards,

34

and the Mayor shot up with all his fingers spread out wide apart, crying, "*Don't anybody move!* My contact lenses have fallen out!"

"Kaaaa – hic!" said Mortimer.

4

Next morning at the Town Hall they were still searching for the Mayor's contact lenses, which had popped out when Seleena sang her top note.

"Do get rid of those robots!" Mr Cutlink grumbled to Barnoff. "They are no help at all. They make more mess than they tidy up."

"Yes, sir. Here's your tea and the Greek dictionary you asked for, sir," said Barnoff, handing him a computer.

"What use is a *computer* to me?"

"Don't forget," said Barnoff, "the Greek professor is coming to lunch. And the supermarket gentleman, Mr Bonnybuy, will be here for morning coffee. Also your free gift from Pollyargos has arrived, sir, with instructions, and as it's rather big I've left it in the car park."

"What is it?" asked the Mayor, groping blindly for his tea. "I can't see a thing till those new lenses arrive from Quick Fit in the High Street."

"Well," said Barnoff, looking out of the window, "it would be hard to say what it is, sir. It might be a statue. But it's all wrapped up and covered with warning signs."

"What do the signs say?"

"They're all in Greek, sir."

In the Jones house, Mrs Jones was rushing about trying to clean and tidy everything, upstairs and downstairs, at the same time.

"Ben," she said, "Do you think you feel equal to getting that new roll of stair carpet out of the attic?"

"If there's no help for it," sighed her husband. "What in the world possessed you to invite a Greek professor just when I've been told to keep calm?"

"Now, I wonder where the stair rods got to?"

Arabel said, "I think Mortimer used them for his wigwam."

"Oh? And then I suppose he stuffed them down that mine of his. We'll have to stick the stair carpet on with Wonderglue. Ben, *could* you be a duck and put sheets on the spare bed? And you'd better get yourself dressed, you aren't presentable."

The doorbell rang.

"Oh, mercy on us," said Mrs Jones, dropping the vacuum cleaner. "Now what?"

She opened the door.

"Good afternoon, Mrs Jones!" said the man outside. "*Rumbury Gazette!* Have you a moment to say a few words about the crack in the next door garden?"

"A moment!" said Mrs Jones. "I could give you the best years of my life!"

In the Mayor's office, Mr Cutlink was trying on his new contact lenses.

"Ahhh!" he sighed. "That's better."

Looking up over the white towel he had spread on his desk, he saw a large man in a check jacket.

"Mr Mayor?" said the large man. "Bonnybuy here! BB to you!" He slapped the Mayor hard on the back, adding, "Bonny's the name and money's my game. And I hear you may have just the very thing for me?"

"Well," said Mr Cutlink, putting back his lenses which had fallen out when Mr BB slapped his back, "a nod is as good as a wink to a willing horse."

"See here, Mr Mayor," went on BB, "I'm marketing a new candy bar in this country. And I've picked your town to try it on. Here's a sample." And he handed Mr Cutlink a chocolate bar in a red and gold wrapper. "The Mortimer bar. Ever hear of it?"

"The name *does* sound familiar," said Mr Cutlink, cautiously.

"Now, what I want, Mr Mayor, is a show-centre for the campaign, a really *big* building. Do you have such a thing in your town?"

"Why, what a coincidence!" said the Mayor. "Better an empty house than a garden full of cows.

Barnoff, can you arrange a viewing of Tower Heights for Mr Bonnybuy?"

"I've a little business tomorrow," said Mr Bonnybuy, looking at his watch, "but I guess I could take it in the next day."

"Tower Heights!" gasped Barnoff, and he dropped the tray he was carrying, with two cups of coffee on it.

Up in Rumbury Park, Seleena had run into trouble. Some indignant mothers were leaving the park, dragging furious children behind them.

"I'm not staying here another minute; it's not safe!" said one angry mum.

Chris, who had just arrived with his guitar, said in surprise to Seleena, "What's she so bothered about?" as the mum looked daggers at Seleena.

"Why, it is quite odd," said Seleena. "I was practising my singing, doing no harm, and – all of a sudden – there was such an enormous crash! Like an earthquake! They say the tropical greenhouse fell into a thousand pieces."

"Nevermore, nevermore," murmured Mortimer, gazing admiringly at Seleena.

"It was quite sad," said Seleena, "but I am sure *I* did not cause it to happen."

"No," said Arabel, "you've got a *lovely* voice!"

"Maybe it was the Rumbury Fault," said Chris.

"And what is that, please?" asked Seleena.

"Why, you see," explained Chris, "the whole borough of Rumbury is built over a great hollow cave. My grandad said he went down there once. They called it the Devil's Ballroom in those days."

"And so," said Seleena, greatly interested, "the whole of Rumbury will one day fall into this ballroom?"

"Oh, I think it's just a story," said Chris. "But when there's a crack in the street, that's what they say."

"There's a crack in the garden next to our house," Arabel reminded Seleena, who cried enthusiastically, "This Rumbury is a mysterious place! I could make up many songs about it!"

"Just don't sing them near any glasshouses," Chris advised.

The Mayor and his personal assistant had gone to take a look at Rumbury Tower Heights before Mr Bonnybuy arrived to inspect the building.

"It does look a bit cracked," said Mr Cutlink, doubtfully. "D'you think there would be time to paint it? Many a cracked bell kills the cat."

"We could offer it as an Ancient Monument," suggested Barnoff.

"And then there's that business of the Rumbury Fault," the Mayor worried on. "No one remembered about that great cave underneath, at the time when the Tower Heights was built. But we don't want to offer Mr Bonnybuy a pig in a poke."

"I think you mean a toad in the hole, sir?" said Barnoff.

In Rumbury Prison, Leggit was growing very impatient.

"Why don't I get an answer from those boys?" he worried, over and over. "I sent them a perfectly plain message, carried by a highly respectable carrier – what are they playing at?"

With a sudden loud thump and crash, Pio Nono came flopping between the bars of the window. He had a black eye, a broken collar, no whistle, and a dirty paper bandage was wrapped round his neck.

"Ooooo! Hoooo!" he remarked sadly.

"Oh? So you're back at last, are you?" snapped Leggit. "Is that a message round your neck?" He unwrapped the paper from the pigeon's neck. It was a long strip of toilet paper. "What's this? 'Property of Rumbury Borough Council'? Is this supposed to be a joke? No lunch for you! And where's your whistle? What happened?"

The pigeon looked sadly up at the picture of Mortimer on Leggit's wall.

"*He* did it, eh? Oh – all right – here's a bit of

bread. But you ought to stand up for yourself," said Leggit. "And where did that paper come from? Don't tell me the Council have got my garden roped off?"

He sat frowning and considering, while the pigeon finished off the bread.

In the Jones house the phone was ringing. The phone stood on a window-sill, halfway up the stairs. Mr Jones was upstairs in the visitor's room, making the bed. Mrs Jones was in the kitchen, washing a huge load of curtains in the newly-repaired washing machine. Neither of them heard the phone.

After a while it stopped ringing.

At the Town Hall, Bill and Joe came dashing into the Mayor's office with their bleepers going full blast.

"Okay, okay boys – just a minute—" said Barnoff. He pointed his remote control at them. The bleeping came to a stop.

"Those gismos are going to give me a heart attack one of these days," gasped Bill.

"Not today, I hope," said Barnoff. "There's several more jobs for you. First, you are to take away the Mayor's robots; he doesn't like them. All they do is mess up the office. And they never did find his lenses. Second, you've to collect the rare cactus collection from the glasshouse in the park, which has collapsed for some reason. It just fell apart."

"I know the feeling," said Joe. "Where do we take the cactuses?"

"Cact*i*," said Barnoff, primly. "You'd better bring them back here. The Mayor hasn't decided what to do with them yet."

For the third time that morning he dialled the Jones number. "Funny – nobody answers . . ."

At Number Six, Rainwater Crescent, Mr and Mrs Jones were now trying to lay the stair carpet. Without stair rods, this was difficult. Ben was up the top, with one bottle of Wonderglue and one end of the carpet; Martha was down at the foot with the other end of the carpet and another bottle of glue. The carpet wanted to roll up again and did so, like lightning, every time somebody let go of it. Mortimer wanted to take a hand with the job, and was only prevented by Arabel holding him tightly round his middle.

"It would be better if you took that bird to play in the garden," panted Mrs Jones.

"There isn't much garden left. The hole's spread to our side now," said Arabel, sadly. However, she carried Mortimer outside. But soon it started to rain.

When the carpet-laying was half done, Mr Jones said, "There's going to be too much carpet left loose in the middle. We're going to have to start again."

So they started again. This meant unsticking the carpet from the stairs at the top and bottom. Once unstuck from the stairs, the carpet wanted to stick to everything else – the banister, the wallpaper, Mrs Jones, the front door, Mr Jones, and itself.

When they were halfway through the second attempt, the phone started ringing. Mr Jones, who was nearest, picked up the receiver, holding a bottle of glue with his other hand, supporting the carpet in mid-air with his foot.

"Jones here," he said.

"Ah, that is Mr Jones, *endaxi,*" said a voice. "Here is Tigran!"

"Well, you'll have to stay at Tigran," said Mr Jones. "Jones taxi is out of service." And he rang off.

"Who was it?" asked Mrs Jones from the stair foot.

"Someone wanted a taxi. From Tigran, wherever that is."

"But, *Ben* – that was the Ancient Greek Professor. His *name* is Tigran!"

Arabel and Mortimer came in, rather wet.

"Don't let that bird near the stairs!" warned Mrs Jones. "They're all over glue. He'd be there for life. And Dad's up at the top and his shoes are stuck to the fifth step."

Very displeased, Mortimer flapped on to the banisters and went up them, beak over claw.

"I think we're going to have to start this job for the third time," sighed Mr Jones . . .

An hour later they were still at it when the doorbell rang.

"I reckon that must be your Professor, Martha," said Mr Jones, looking out of the staircase window, beside which he happened to be standing. "You'll have to go, my shoes are still stuck to the fifth step."

"Oh, no! My hands are all over glue!" wailed Mrs Jones. "Arabel, dearie, *you* go. Make a nice curtsey and say *kalamari* to the gentleman."

"All right, Ma," said Arabel.

She opened the front door. Outside stood an elderly man with a long, white beard. He carried a small suitcase and was looking with interest at the huge hole.

"Kalamari," Arabel greeted him politely.

Professor Tigran looked a little puzzled.

"Squids?" he said.

"Bless you," said Arabel, who thought that he had sneezed. "Are you the Greek Professor? Would you like to come in?"

However, as she stepped aside to let the Professor into the house, they heard a series of terrific thumps from inside.

The carpet had finally pulled itself loose, rolled

itself up, and now came bounding down the stairs. They just had time to leap out of the way before it shot through the front door, crashed through the fence, and plunged into the hole in Leggit's garden.

Mortimer came bouncing out too, but he was caught just in time by Arabel.

"Nevermore!" he shouted joyfully.

"*Oimoi!*" exclaimed the Professor, throwing up his hands in amazement. "Ghwhat does this mean?"

5

By next morning, Professor Tigran and the Jones
family had settled down quite comfortably together.
Professor Tigran was asking: "And Mrs Jones, in your
household ghis there a Matrilineal Moiety?"

"I'm afraid not, Professor; but we can offer you
some rolled oats? Or some seed cake?"

"Thank you Mrs Jones; I will ghave only a cup of
coffee. In my country we eat later."

"Oh, we eat later as well! This is only breakfast."

The phone rang, and Mrs Jones went to answer it.
Mortimer was happily slinging round his head a
string of red wooden worry-beads which the
Professor had given him. At this moment they flew
into the toaster.

"And does your raven foretell the future?"
Professor Tigran asked Mr Jones.

Mrs Jones came back, crying, "Well! Guess what!
The Mayor has come down off his high horse!"

The toaster shot up, scattering red worry-beads
over the breakfast table.

Mr Jones said, threateningly, "That raven, Professor,
has no *idea* of what's going to happen if I get my hands
on him. What's this about the Town Hall, Martha?"

"The Mayor has had an accident?" inquired Professor Tigran.

"Only a figure of speech, Professor. They want me to go and lend a hand in the Mayor's office. Ben and our Arabel will look after you, Mr Tigran."

"*Yassoo,* Mrs Jones," said the Professor, standing up and bowing.

"You ought to take something for that cold," said Mrs Jones, putting on her coat.

She went out of the front door, but came back in a moment to say, "There's a flood now, outside! This is the last straw! They'd better send round that nice lady plumber. At least *she's* a port in a storm!"

"I think I'd rather drown," said Mr Jones, sadly.

Out in Rainwater Crescent, Bill and Joe were directing the Mayor's robots towards the hole in Leggit's garden, which now had a quantity of water in the bottom.

"Hey, this is *fun*!" said Bill. One of the robots looked at him pleadingly.

"It's a long way – to tip a robot—" sang Joe.

Have-a-Go Flo came up behind the boys, pulling Professor Tigran's trunk on wheels behind her.

"Wotcher, boys!" she called.

Both boys spun round. One of the robots toppled into the hole.

"Ooh, I'm sorry about that!" exclaimed Flo, peering down. "But we can get it out again if you want it?"

"Nah, don't bother," said Joe. "They were due to be scrapped. They gave his Worship the fantods. Is that trunk to go down as well?"

"No, no," said Flo, "that's for the Joneses' lodger."

And she wheeled the trunk towards the doorway of Number Six. Mortimer, who had been watching through the window, came out eagerly to lend a hand.

In Rumbury Jail, Mr Leggit was becoming impatient and morose. This was because he had found a copy of the *Rumbury Gazette* in the prison library.

IS RUMBURY CRACKING UP? he read. MAYOR SAYS BILL WILL BE ASTRONOMICAL.

"Humph!" he muttered. "It was. They sent it to *me*."

THEY MAY HAVE TO TUNNEL BENEATH LEGS OF TOWER HEIGHTS WITHOUT UPSETTING THE FOUNDATIONS.

"Hey! – I can send a message!"

Glancing round, Leggit snatched out a page of the newspaper and stuffed it inside his prison T-shirt. Back in his cell, he underlined the words *Bill – tunnel*

– *legs* – *out*, rolled the paper up tightly, and passed it to Pio Nono.

"Now, you carry this to Bill – or Joe, it doesn't matter which – and this time, *bring me back an answer!*"

"Ooooo," said the pigeon gloomily.

At Rumbury Town Hall, the Mayor's office was now filled up with cacti. The Council Dog did not like them at all. He was already sneezing from prickles up his nose.

The Mayor was looking out of the window, between green bulges and spines and prickles.

"Barnoff!" he called. "What's become of the Greek Gift? Where's it gone?"

"That's all right, sir," said Barnoff coming in. "I had the signs translated, and moved it somewhere safer than the car park."

"Those Greek signs? What did they say?"

"*Keep in Open Air*, sir, and *Do Not Thump or Kick*. I put the Gift in the children's playground."

"But they'll all thump and kick it," the Mayor said anxiously.

"No, sir. They can't read."

Mrs Jones burst in, very cross, with a mop and duster.

"Those cactuses!" she said. "I certainly didn't

50

bargain for *them* when I said I'd be your domestic conciliator."

With her duster she aimed a swipe at a Prickly Pear.

"Mrs Jones, please!" cried the Mayor. "The one that you're poking now is a rare Saguaro, thousands of years old. It is almost extinct! It can only be pollinated by bats!"

"I say, now, that's a thought," said Barnoff. "There's that colony of bats up at the Tower Heights; perhaps we could put the cacti up there, bring them all together?"

The Council Dog wagged his tail joyfully, and knocked a large, potted, knotted tangle on to the Mayor's desk, scattering earth and prickles.

"Either those prehistoric pests go – or I give in my notice!" announced Mrs Jones.

"Humph!" said the Mayor. "Barnoff, you'd better call Bill and Joe."

Barnoff pointed his control towards the window.

At Number Six, Rainwater Crescent, they were busy hoisting Professor Tigran's trunk out of the hole in Leggit's garden.

"There you are, sir," said Have-a-Go Flo. "Right as rain!"

She opened the lid and looked inside.

"Well – anyway – I can easily have the water pumped out for you. I can't think how it happened to fall down into that hole."

"*I've* got plenty of ideas," grumbled Mr Jones, looking at Mortimer.

"I'm very sorry your books got wet, Professor," said Arabel.

Mortimer took a flying leap into the Professor's trunk. A lot of water slopped out.

"Stop that, Mortimer!" yelled Mr Jones.

"Ah, no! Zis is most intelligent," said the Professor. "Archimedes's principle. Raven goes in – equivalent wvater comes out. I must study zis bird's thought processes."

"A life's work!" muttered Mr Jones, mopping himself.

Bill and Joe toiled slowly along Rainwater Crescent with a trolley-load of cacti.

"Hey!" said Bill, when they had gone a little way down the street. "Blow taking these all the way up to Rumbury Tower Heights. Why don't we just dump them all down Leggy's hole? What the eye don't see—"

"– Is worth a bird in the bush," said Joe.

They tipped a lot of the cacti down the hole in Leggit's garden, but some of the load went over the fence into the Joneses' garden.

"Oh, well," said Joe, "we'll take care of those later. I need a coffee. And *Socksy Boy* is on at the Rumbury Metro."

"Let's go," said Bill. Off they went.

Inside Number Six, Mr Jones and the Professor were drinking tea, while they waited for the contents of the Professor's trunk to dry off.

Mr Jones was saying, "If *kalimera* is good morning, and *kalispera* is good evening, what do you Greeks say in the afternoon?"

"Ah," said the Professor, "in Greece zere is no good afternoon, because everybody takes siesta."

A tremendous noise of pumping, crashing, creaking and throbbing started up in front of the house. Have-a-Go Flo was out in the street with a truck, a pump, and about a hundred metres of yellow hose-pipe. She was pumping water out of the hole in Leggit's garden.

Pio Nono the pigeon came flying along the street, grasping a newspaper scroll in his claw. Seeing Flo's truck he hovered, puzzled, then perched on a cactus which had been left dangling over the edge of the hole.

"Oooo!" said the pigeon.

"Yoo-hoo!" said Flo, turning round in surprise. "Who are *you*?"

But at that moment the cactus, with the pigeon clutching it, fell into the hole.

"Funny," said Flo, scratching her red head, "for a moment I thought someone might be trying to send me a message."

In the Town Hall, Mr Cutlink was looking at a fax which he had just received from Mr Bonnybuy. "*En route for Tokyo*," began the fax.

"Oh, no!" cried Mr Cutlink in anguish. "We've lost him."

"Go on reading," said Barnoff. The fax was so long that one end of it trailed out through the office door, and the Council Dog sat on it. The paper was even longer than the Joneses' stair carpet.

"En route for Tokyo, flew over Rumbury Town, looked out the window, and saw this *great* building on legs. (Drawing enclosed.) If it's for sale, don't accept any offers till I return."

The drawing, unmistakeably that of Rumbury Tower Heights, legs and all, was so long that it took up most of the fax.

"But when *will* he return?" wailed Mr Cutlink.

"Maybe it says at the bottom," pointed out Barnoff.

At the foot of the fax – when it was pulled out from under the Council Dog – they found, "Back

Tuesday. All the best from Bonnybuy," and a scrawled signature.

"But that's fantastic!" said the Mayor. "Quite fantastic. If he buys it we can afford to fix the hole in Rainwater Crescent. Better a mouse in the hand than a horse in the bush. Now the next thing we have to do is contact Professor Tigran and find out what he has in mind for his Gift Unveiling Ceremony. I hope he doesn't want national dances in costume. All we've got are Council overalls."

"Could we hold the Gift Unveiling Ceremony on the same day as the Song Contest, sir?"

"Good thinking, Barnoff – then we need only pay the town band once. A penny saved keeps the cat away."

There was trouble up in the park. A lot of angry mothers were demonstrating about the veiled Greek Gift which Barnoff had deposited in the middle of the children's playground. The mums carried signs which said: THE GREEK THING MUST GO. BEWARE OF GREEK GIFTS. DON'T DUMP WRAPPED OBJECTS IN OUR PARK!

They were also protesting against all the different groups who were busy practising their songs in the park. So some of the signs carried by mothers said: FIVE MINUTES' PEACE, PLEASE! FIVE

MINUTES' PEACE! LESS HULLABALOO! FEWER SONGS!

As they were all chanting their slogans together the messages got mixed up: "Don't dump five-minute objects. Fewer Greek things. Five minutes' hullabaloo."

Chris and Arabel were going back to Rainwater Crescent after a visit to the supermarket to buy Greek food. Taking a short cut through the park they were amazed to hear all these protests.

"What's happening?" said Arabel.

"They say they want five minutes' peace – but they aren't helping much," said Chris.

Mortimer, who was riding in the trolley on a load of garlic, tomatoes, cucumbers, pots of yoghurt, bunches of grapes, and bottles of olive oil, reached out and tried to grab the placard of a mum who was walking past. It said: FEWER SONGS IN OUR PARK!

"No, Mortimer, that's not your sign. You must let go," said Arabel.

"Why," cried the mum, "There are some of those singers *now*! Look, he's got a guitar hidden under all those tomatoes. Hoodlums! Hippies! Leave our park in peace!"

Mortimer flung a tomato at the mum with such force that the trolley he was in started rolling away down the hill.

"Oh, come on, Arabel. Let's get out of here," called Chris, racing after the trolley.

In the front garden of Number Six, Rainwater Crescent, Mr Jones and Professor Tigran were staring in wonder at a huge pile of cacti which had been dumped beside the hole in Leggit's garden. The fence had collapsed under their weight, so they were spilling across into the Jones garden.

"Very queer, indeed," said Mr Jones. "They weren't there this morning."

"Ghow can zey ghave come to be ghere?" inquired the Professor.

Mrs Jones, just arriving home from work at the Town Hall, opened the gate and let out a shriek at sight of the cacti.

"Ben Jones! You haven't been and gone and spent all my earnings on those bat-eating prickly pear-apples?"

"You are familiar wviz zese plants, Mrs Jones?" asked the Professor.

"Wouldn't touch them with a barge pole," said Mrs Jones. "How, pray, did they get from the Town Hall into my garden?"

Mortimer came sailing down Rainwater Crescent in a supermarket trolley loaded with cucumbers and tomatoes.

"Help!" cried Mrs Jones as he cannoned into her. And she fell backwards into the cacti.

6

At breakfast next morning, Mrs Jones was all covered in scratches from the cactus prickles she had fallen into, and bandages over the scratches.

"You zhould put ghoney on zhose scratches, Mrs Jones," said the Professor, sympathetically. "Zhen zey wvill soon cease to ghurt."

"Thanks, Professor. I'll try that. Have you any good advice about Mr Jones's high blood-pressure?"

"Ghe should think about a running river. Also use worry-beads," said the Professor, producing a string of amber ones from his pocket and passing them to Mr Jones, who began peacefully fiddling with them, and started to look better right away.

"Lucky Mortimer's out of the house or he'd want them," said Mrs Jones.

"Wvat is zis bird's main function, Mrs Jones? Is he ze totem or emblem of your family?"

"I dunno about emblem," said Mrs Jones, a little puzzled. "He's more of an embarrassment than an emblem."

"And his main function?"

"Putting things down that hole, it seems to be, just now."

In the front garden Mortimer was busy hurling cacti into the deep hole.

"For once," said Mr Jones, "he's being useful."

Mrs Jones went into the lounge and let out a fearful wail.

"Martha! What's up?" gasped her husband, rushing after her. Professor Tigran followed, pulling out yet another set of worry-beads.

With a hand that shook like a flag in a breeze, Mrs Jones pointed at the fireplace. Right in the middle of the mantelpiece, running up to the ceiling and down to the fender, was a great zigzag crack, like a lightning flash.

"This house is hoaxed! Jinxed! Fated!" gasped Mrs Jones.

"But zis is a sign from Fate – an oracle!" cried Professor Tigran, all excited. "I was about to invite your daughter and raven to perform ze Unwrapping Rite on my Gift Statue from Pollyargos. Zis is proof zhat I have chosen rightly."

"Write on the statue? Wouldn't that be graffiti?" said Mrs Jones, puzzled.

"No, no, Mrs Jones; I zhink great good fortune will fall on your house."

"If anything else falls on it," said Mr Jones, "we'll have to move."

There was a crash as Mortimer swung in through

his raven-flap and came to find out what was happening. As soon as he saw the crack in the wall, he dived into it, head first. Out of the crack poured a tremendous cloud of soot.

In the street, Bill and Joe were greatly perplexed.

"Who'd pinch two dozen cacti?" grumbled Joe. "Just because we went to the pictures?"

"Can't see a thing below there; it's all black," said Bill, peering down the hole. "Ooooh!" as the pigeon came fluttering out. Pio Nono still carried a tattered scroll of newspaper. He proffered it to Bill.

"It's from Leggy," said Bill, frowning as he peered at it. "A piece of an evening paper. Words have been underlined. Bill – tunnel – legs – out."

"You mean," said Joe, "we've got to get all that stuff *out* again? Dig a tunnel to the jail for Legs to escape? This is worse than the Council job!"

"Well – s'pose we'd better make a start," said Bill glumly.

"It's getting real deep down there. We'll need a ladder."

"I reckon you earned a handout," Bill told the pigeon. "I got a free gift at the shopping centre. It's called a Mortimer bar."

"Coo!" said the pigeon, eagerly snatching the bar.

But at that moment he was mysteriously yanked back down the hole, Mortimer bar and all.

At the Town Hall, Mrs Jones bustled into the Mayor's office with a can of spray.

"Did you know, Mr Cutlink, that those cactuses had *fleas*? I've come out in a rash. I'm going to give this place a good turn-out!" she announced.

"Oh, blimey!" said the Mayor. "Perhaps you've got an allergy. Rub it with a dock leaf."

"Never mind that. This room needs a thorough spring-clean."

"In that case," said the Mayor, "I'll go and see Professor Tigran at your house. I've tried to call him several times but I can't seem to get through on the phone."

"It's off the hook," Mrs Jones explained, "so that Ben can get a bit of peace and quiet."

"Lucky man," sighed Cutlink. "If you keep your bed in the bank, nobody can steal it."

"And high time you did take a look at our house, Mr Cutlink, if I may say so; it's in a *disgraceful* state!" Mrs Jones called after him as he left.

In the Jones house, the Professor was helping Mr Jones with some Greek cookery.

"Olive oil – garlic – mint – yoghurt – zese you

must have in *all* Greek food—"

Arabel came in, looking anxious. "Pa, have you seen Mortimer anywhere – is he still in the crack?"

"Maybe he went all the way down to the Devil's Ballroom," suggested Mr Jones, gloomily. "That crack probably reaches down there."

"Ze Devil's Ballroom? *Oreste?* Wvat is zis?" inquired the Professor.

The doorbell rang. "You go, dearie," said Mr Jones. "I'm reeking of garlic." To the Professor he explained, "The Devil's Ballroom is an underground cave below this town."

Arabel came back with Seleena.

"I think I must have been sent to your stricken town for a purpose!" the Professor was exclaiming, excitedly.

"Pa," said Arabel, "this is Seleena."

"Arabel's told us all about your singing, Miss Seleena," said Mr Jones. "Pleased to meet you."

Seleena and the Professor bowed to each other.

Have-a-Go Flo poked her head round the back door.

"Hey-o, Mr Jones!" she said. "Mrs J told me about the crack in your mantel. Can I take a look at it?"

Without waiting for an answer, she looked through the door to the lounge and said, "Croopus!"

The front-door bell rang again.

"I see that you are the hub of the universe, Mr Jones!" said the Professor.

"Makes a change from Cabby of the Year, I s'pose," sighed Mr Jones.

Arabel came back from the front door. "This time it's the Mayor, Pa," she said.

Mr Cutlink, with Barnoff, squeezed into the kitchen, which was quite full by now.

"About the hole in the garden, is it, your Worship?" said Mr Jones, a bit flustered by all this company.

"Ah, no, not today," said the Mayor. "It is about the Gift Ceremony. We need to make the arrangements with the Professor."

"I am wvriting ze speech now," the Professor told Cutlink. "Ze little girl and raven wvill play important part—"

Both Mr Jones and the Mayor looked extremely doubtful at this.

"Shall I take you to the park, Arabel?" said Seleena, feeling there were rather too many people in the room.

"Yes, please – if only we can find Mortimer," said Arabel.

"Maybe I sing – and then he will come out from where he is hiding!" offered Seleena.

She sang and the Mayor's lenses fell out, but Mortimer did not appear.

Bill and Joe had helped themselves to a ladder from somebody's shed and were exploring the deep hole in Leggit's garden. Joe held the ladder at the top, while Bill, down below, poked nervously about.

But all of a sudden Bill let out a yell and came panting and scrambling up the ladder, with his hair, what there was of it, standing up in spikes.

He gulped: "There's something *down* there!"

"We know there is, dumb-bell! We put most of it in!"

"But this was *alive*! Honest! And it spoke!"

"What? Hey, let's get out of here!"

Barnoff, Professor Tigran, and the Mayor had left Number Six, Rainwater Crescent and gone off to wait for Mr Bonnybuy at Rumbury Tower Heights. Barnoff had arranged for the legs of the tower to be decorated with orange traffic tape.

"Makes it look a bit more cheerful," sighed the Mayor. "Now keep your fingers crossed, Barnoff, here comes Mr B."

A huge black car pulled up, and Mr Bonnybuy shot out, manhandling a camera the size of a lawn-mower, which ran on its own trolley.

"Wow!" said Mr Bonnybuy, looking at Tower Heights. "Now – this – is – *big*! This thing could be worth *money*!"

He began taking dozens of pictures of the building from every side, while Barnoff and the Mayor followed him about, hoping that he wouldn't notice the cracks and the peeling plaster.

"What the eye doesn't see can't be put in old bottles," whispered the Mayor to Barnoff.

Professor Tigran, wandering away from them, walked across the open space to inspect his Gift, which Barnoff had left for the time being in the children's playground.

The Gift was still done up in its wrappings, but these had partly come off as it was carted through Rumbury Town. It had orange tape looped about it, and various signs, some in Greek (which nobody understood) and some in English which said: *Don't Kick*, *Don't Thump*, and *Post No Bills*.

The surface of the Gift, where it could be seen through holes in the wrapping, was rough, like rock, and some of it seemed to be black, while some was white. It was about the size of a garden shed, but no particular shape. It resembled one of Mr Jones's lumps of dough, which had been squeezed about a bit.

"Ex – cell – ent! It ghas travelled wvell!" said the Professor, pleased.

"What *is* it?" asked Arabel, who had come to the playground with Seleena. "I mean, what is it made of?"

"It is Negative Poisson Ratio rock."

"What's that?"

"It grows thicker and thicker when stretched." (What the Professor actually said was "sicker and sicker".) "If a missile should hit it, it wvill expand in all directions!" added the Professor, proudly.

The Mayor, Barnoff, and Mr Bonnybuy were still walking round the Tower Heights building taking pictures, when they heard the sound of singing from the playground.

"Is that local folk-singing?" asked Mr BB, much impressed. "Wonderful lot of talent you got here, Mr Mayor!"

"Birds of a feather sing louder than worms," said Cutlink.

At that moment Seleena, in the playground, hit a tremendous top note. A huge cloud of bats whooshed out from various holes in the top of the tower building and wheeled about overhead. There were so many that they blackened the sky like a dust-storm.

"Jeepers! Do you have tornados here too?" cried Mr Bonny, staring upwards.

"Barnoff!" said the Mayor severely. "Didn't you tell Mr Bonny about the special effects?"

"I – I thought it would be nice to leave it as a surprise for him, sir," said Barnoff, with great presence of mind.

In Rainwater Crescent, Have-a-Go Flo was striding past the huge hole in Leggit's garden. Noticing the top of the ladder sticking out, she looked down into the hole and called, "Yoo-hoo? Bill? Joe? You down there?"

The ladder shot out like a javelin.

Have-a-Go Flo, not usually taken by surprise, let out a shriek. Then she raced up the path to the Jones house, shouting, "Mr Jones, Mr Jones!"

Arabel and Professor Tigran were walking slowly back from the park. At the top of Rainwater Crescent they met Mrs Jones, bustling home from the Town Hall.

"What's up, dearie?" asked Mrs Jones, noticing at once that her daughter looked very anxious.

"It's Mortimer, Ma. He's still missing. There were a lot of bats in the park but we didn't find him."

"I am zhure, my dear, zat ghe wvill be at ghome, no? Zis raven knows where his bed is buttered," said the Professor, kindly.

At the front gate of their garden they found Mr

Jones, looking highly disturbed. "Arabel! Martha! Don't go near that hole!"

"There's something down below there!" chimed in Have-a-Go Flo, coming up beside him.

"Indeed, indeed, zis is a most lucky drama!" exclaimed the Professor, peering hopefully at the hole. "A bandersnatch, maybe?"

Pio Nono shot out of the hole, like a bolt from a crossbow.

"*Eene epeegon* – an emergency!" cried the Professor.

"No, a pigeon," corrected Mr Jones.

"But a pigeon couldn't have tossed out a ladder," argued Have-a-Go Flo.

"Could Mortimer be down there too?"

As Arabel said this, Mortimer himself hurtled backwards out of the hole, covered in soot and honey, and with his feathers all on end. Arabel just managed to catch him as he shot by.

"Mercy on us!" cried Mrs Jones. "It must be those man-eating, hair-raising plants down there, wreaking their revenge!"

7

Next day in the Town Hall the Mayor was
auditioning Bill and Joe, who sang:

"He's black and I'm white
But we're covered in plasters
So we both look a sight
We're working all day, just to get the job done
It may be very healthy – but it isn't much fun
Saturday night and we're taking out plants
Send reinforcements, we're going to a dance!"

They hopped around the office, wailing and
clutching the bandages that covered all their cactus
wounds. The Council Dog howled mournfully,
perhaps in sympathy.

"Well," said the Mayor, looking uncertain, "I can't
say it's my cup of tea – *or* the dog's – but I suppose it's
what goes, these days. A song is as good as a shoe to
a deaf horse."

"So, do we get to be in the contest?" asked Bill
eagerly.

"Due to a severe shortage of entries – yes,"
admitted the Mayor. "But I want that song longer –
and better."

Mrs Jones burst in as Bill and Joe left.

"I'm going on lie-down strike!" she said. "Here I shall stay, lying on the floor of this office, until steps are taken!" And she lay down.

"Steps?" said the Mayor faintly. "*Whose* steps?"

"The stepladder!" said Mrs Jones. "The stepladder that some hoodoo flung out of that great hole into our garden. And what about the crack in our mantel?"

"Keystone under the hearth, keystone under the horse!" announced the Mayor, confusingly. "The Council Dog needs an airing, Mrs Jones, and I think he caught fleas from the cacti. Would you be so kind as to take him to the vet?"

Mrs Jones was so taken aback that she got up and led the Council Dog out of the office.

In Rainwater Crescent, Arabel had put up a scarecrow beside the huge hole. It was dressed in her father's old taxi-driving overcoat and cap.

"There, Mortimer!" she said.

"Kaaark!" said Mortimer, much interested.

Professor Tigran was interested too. "Is to scare birds, yes?" he said.

"Well, not Mortimer," said Arabel. "But that pigeon that keeps coming – Mortimer doesn't like him trespassing in his mine."

Mr Jones came out.

"I'm off to see the doctor," he said. "Can you hold the fort here, Professor?"

"*Endaxi!* I do zis! I am needing to talk to your daughter and raven about ze Gift Ceremony, Mr Jones."

And, as Mr Jones hurried away up Rainwater Crescent, the Professor said to Arabel, "I ghave brought from Pollyargos a large baton – you say baton?"

"What is that?" said Arabel, puzzled.

"Is a gong-stick – you say gong-stick? Wviv wvich to beat on gong?"

"Oh, a gong-stick, yes?"

"I wvould like very much for you to read a little speech wvile Mortimer strikes zree times wviv gong-stick."

"Kaaark!" said Mortimer, greatly pleased.

"He'll like that," agreed Arabel.

"Zhen I get out ze gong-stick, and we practise," said the Professor.

In the Mayor's office, Barnoff said to Mr Cutlink, "That was a stroke of genius, sir, sending Mrs Jones out with the Council Dog."

"Never drown a dog when you can see the shore," said the Mayor. "Is there any news from Bonnybuy about the Heights?"

"He's still consulting with his marketing managers. Pity about those bats. I hope they didn't put him off."

"Pity about the *singing*. I wish I'd never planned this wretched contest; it's brought nothing but trouble. First that girl made my lenses fall out, then she wakes up the bats."

"Seleena, sir?" said Barnoff. "I've got an idea – maybe we could get her to lead the bats out of the Tower – Pied Piper technique?"

"But then," said the Mayor, "where would we *put* the bats? Meanwhile, Barnoff, you'd better get round to Rainwater Crescent and put up some signs."

"What for, sir?"

"To make it look as if we're doing something about the hole before Mrs Jones gets home. – By the way, what about Leggit? Did he ever pay his bill?"

"No, sir. But how's he supposed to get the money while he's in prison?"

"That's *his* problem," said the Mayor. "Cracked jugs don't cry over spilt milk."

Bill and Joe had gone back to take another look at the hole in Leggit's garden.

"*Fine* idea of yours," said Joe bitterly, "to spend our day off tunnelling into Rumbury Jail."

"Not my idea," said Bill, "it was Leggy's. – Hey, hush, look behind you!"

Bill turned to see Barnoff, tottering under the weight of several traffic cones which he wore on his head, as well as bundles of orange traffic tape, and a road-mender's tent.

"Hallo, boys," he said. "Thought this was your day off?"

"Just on our way to the park," said Bill, hastily.

"I don't suppose you'd see your way to give me a hand? Got to get this hole screened somehow."

"Why, of course we'd be *glad* to help," said Bill, kicking Joe on the shin. "Wouldn't we, Joe?"

In the Jones kitchen, Professor Tigran had been giving Mortimer some practice with a large gong-stick. It was made of wood, about the length of a broom, with one end heavily weighted and wrapped in leather. Mortimer loved it.

The practice had led to various objects being knocked over, and some broken.

"Perhaps we had better play some other game," suggested Arabel, panting, after a while. She put the gong-stick in the other room.

So now the Professor was teaching Mortimer to count to three.

"Ghere are zree apples in a row," he said, arranging them on the kitchen table. "Vun, tvo, zree. Mortimer, you see? Zis is *vun*, zis is *tvo*, zis is *zree*."

"Nevermore!" cried Mortimer, and ate the third apple.

"*Ex – cell – ent!*" cried the Professor.

Mr Jones came back from his visit to the doctor.

"And ghow vas the Doctor, Mr Jones?"

Mr Jones looked puzzled. "He can't find anything wrong with me."

"Just as I ghave said, it is all ze feeling," the Professor told him. "After ghappy time at ghome wvif family, you feel all better."

Mortimer, who had gone into the other room, returned dragging his gong-stick and dropped it on Mr Jones's foot.

"*Moses!*" exclaimed Mr Jones, leaping eighteen centimetres into the air. "What's that?"

Out in Rainwater Crescent Bill and Joe, having put up a red-and-white striped workmen's tent to hide the hole in Leggit's garden, were admiring their handiwork.

"Looks nice, dunnit?" said Bill.

"Shall we light a fire and roast chestnuts?" said Joe.

"Did you bring some?"

"Nah."

"*Boo!*" said Leggit, suddenly popping his head out of the tent.

Both boys screamed, clutched each other, and fell over backwards.

"Mercy! Murder!"

"Don't *be* like that!" said Leggit, crossly. "I've come all this way to see you two; you might give me a bit of welcome. I must say, that was a brilliant idea of yours, sending those robots to help me. I'd never have thought you had it in you. But the lights are failing on one of them. I reckon his batteries are low."

"You mean they dug along all the way to the *prison*?" said Joe, amazed.

"Dug you *out*?" said Bill.

Leggit nodded. "I left one in my cell. He's got my clothes on. I daresay no one will notice the difference till *his* batteries run out. But now I need a coat – ah, that will do." He took Mr Jones's taxi-driving coat and cap off the scarecrow.

"And I'd like a bite to eat, and something for the bird. Yoo hoo? Where are you?" He stuck his head back into the tent.

"And have you got some money for me?" he called over his shoulder.

Bill and Joe stared at each other.

"Ooops," said Bill. "He wanted money – dough for hole – that's what he meant in his message!"

"We mustn't get mixed up in anything dicey now," Joe told Leggit. "See, we've gone straight. A few more weeks and we're in the clear. We can't blow it now."

"We work for the Council!" Bill said, proudly.

"Oh, well, never mind," said Leggit. "I haven't been wasting my time in jail. Pio Nono here—" he patted the pigeon who was sitting on his shoulder, "– is now a trained hypnotist, and he's going to work on that meddlesome black bird next door. I'll make the raven rob the bank; he's bound to be caught – but not till *I've* got the cash, ha! ha!"

"Coo!" said Bill.

"Coo," said Pio Nono.

"Hey!" cried Joe. "Somebody's coming! Quick – let us in the tent."

Mrs Jones, trudging wearily along Rainwater Crescent, said to Seleena, who was kindly carrying her groceries: "Thanks *ever* so much, dear, and for your help with that dratted dog. It's just wonderful what singing will do to animals. This is my house where I live."

"Yes, I have already met your daughter," said Seleena. "Such a delightful girl. And your raven, of course."

"Yes, they are a pair, aren't they," said Mrs Jones proudly. "Well, so long . . ."

In her kitchen Mrs Jones found her husband, Arabel, and the Professor as well as Mortimer, who was sitting with a row of three boiled eggs before him on the table. Mortimer pointed his beak at each egg in turn, then leaned forward and swallowed the third egg, eggcup and all.

"Zis is most, *most* intelligent," said the Professor, approvingly.

Mrs Jones sank into a chair.

"Here, Martha – a nice hot cup of tea is what *you* need," said Mr Jones, pouring her one. "How did you get on at the Town Hall today?"

"I've never been so insatiated in my life!" said Mrs Jones crossly, gulping the tea. "Making me take that Dog for a walk! I'd rather be dragged across the Alps by my tongue. If it wasn't for that nice girl—"

"You'd better give up the Town Hall job, Martha. I'll get the old cab out tomorrow. The doctor says I'm going on nicely," said her husband.

"*Ben!* You can't do that! I don't trust these miracle cures. And I certainly shan't give that Mayor the pleasure of my notice until my time is up."

"I think *my* time will be up by then," said Mr Jones, gloomily.

Mortimer counted up Mr Jones's numerous pill-bottles on the table, then swallowed the third one.

"Hey! Stop that!" shouted Mr Jones.

"He's counting up to three, don't you see," said Arabel.

"Mortimer – *out*!" cried Mrs Jones. Sulkily,

Mortimer retired through his raven-flap.

Outside in the dusk, Leggit, in his red-and-white striped tent, was inspecting a bag of provisions the boys had brought him.

"Hmm, not so bad – the lads have done old Leggit proud," he murmured; "new whistle for the bird, ham sandwich, torch, packet of plasters for the prickles, very thoughtful."

"Coo!" said the pigeon, looking nervously towards the entrance.

"What's up, birdie?"

Squinting through the flap, Leggit observed Mortimer giving the tent an interested survey.

"Wonderful!" hissed Leggit. "The missing link! Walking right into our hands! Where's that whistle, Pio, now's your chance!"

Wearing the new whistle, Pio Nono edged outside the tent and came face to face with Mortimer, who had picked up a traffic cone and was balancing it thoughtfully on his head.

Nervously and shakily, the pigeon played the tune that Leggit had taught him.

*Tootle, toot*le, *too,* too. *Tootle, toot*le, *too,* too.

Interested, beguiled, Mortimer came closer and closer . . .

In the Jones kitchen, the family were startled and unnerved to hear a huge crash from the garden, followed by a number of rumbles and crumbles and smaller crashes.

"*Now* what's happened?" said Mr Jones.

"Oh, Mortimer!" exclaimed Arabel, jumping up anxiously. "Is that you?"

8

By next day, the Jones garden was full of flashing lights and red tape. Mortimer had been rescued from the mine, and, like Mrs Jones, was now covered with sticking-plaster.

"Oh, well, I suppose I'd best be off to the Town Hall," sighed Mrs Jones after breakfast. "No one can say misfortune makes *me* shirk my duties."

"Ah, Mrs Jones," said the Professor. "Can you tell Mayor Cutlink zat ze moon wvill be auspicious for ze Gift Ceremony in four days' time?"

"I'm going back to bed," grumbled Mr Jones. "All this excitement is too much for me."

"I'll come and practise my speech with you, Pa," said Arabel.

He nodded resignedly.

In the Town Hall, two angry mothers were calling on the Mayor.

"We've come to protest about that nasty thing in the park," they told Mr Cutlink. "The Rumbury Mothers have donated twenty benches, hand-made from recycled products, for the use of persons needing five minutes' peace. To make room for them, that Thing has to go . . ."

They shook their shopping bags at the Mayor, then swept out angrily.

"Oh, dear," said Mr Cutlink. "Isn't today the day we are supposed to hear from Bonnybuy?"

Mrs Jones bustled in.

"Good morning, your Mayorship! If you'd like to pop out and do something useful, I'll give this place a good rub-over."

"We're expecting a visitor soon, Mrs Jones," said the Mayor, hastily preparing to leave. "If you could get in some snacks and make the place look welcoming – half a loaf at home is worth a cake in the manger—"

"Ooh, a party, are you having?" said Mrs Jones, pleased. "That's nice."

In Rainwater Crescent, Leggit and his pigeon, both covered in bandages, were being brought their breakfast by Bill and Joe.

"So," said Joe, "your plan didn't work so well? Hypnotising the raven?"

"That brute must be tone deaf," grumbled Leggit. "But we'll have another go."

Bill brought a cup of tea he had been kindly given by Professor Tigran.

"Only one cup?" said Joe.

"Well," said Bill, "I could hardly ask for two more. 'My mate's just chatting up an escaped convict in your garden!'"

"I wouldn't *be* an escaped convict if it weren't for those perishing Joneses and their prying pet," snarled Leggit. "*They* haven't been told to pay a huge bill for the hole. And some of it's in their garden now."

"They're in with the Town Hall lot," said Bill. "Mrs Jones cleans up there, and the Mayor has offloaded some old Professor to their house as well."

"Much use that is to me," grumbled Leggit.

"Well," Joe told him, "Bill and me are going in for the Rumbury Song Contest. If we win, then we can help you out."

"Out of this hole would be a start," said Leggit.

"Would you like to hear our song?" said Bill.

"No thanks! I mean, another time. Come back after dark," said Leggit, hastily.

In the Jones house, Professor Tigran was putting Mr Jones into a trance. They were sitting opposite each other at the kitchen table. Arabel had draped her father's shoulders with a blanket.

"You are vairry, vairry sleeeeepy, Mr Jones," said the Professor. "Only ghappy thoughts fill your ghead

83

. . . beauuuuuuutiful dreams . . . you wvill sleep comfortably until I wvake you . . ."

"Is that magic, Professor?" asked Arabel, as her father's eyes closed.

"No, no, my dear. Just simple medicine. Now ghe wvill rest and not wvorry."

"We could take Mortimer to the park while he sleeps," said Arabel.

"Endaxi!" said the Professor.

In the park, Arabel and Professor Tigran found a lot of mothers protesting about the Gift. They carried placards and shouted slogans.

"But wvat is zis?" cried the Professor in distress. "They do not like my statue – but ghwhy?"

Arabel explained to the mothers: "This is Professor Tigran from Pollyargos. He knows all about the statue. He brought it as a present."

"Well," said a mum, "you can tell him it's not wanted. It's brought nothing but aggravation. It's in the way where it is."

"Ladies, ladies," said the Professor, "may I explain? Zings are not always as zey seem. I wvill explain by telling you ze Greek parable of ze tortoise and ze blackbird—"

The mothers settled down on their benches to listen.

84

Arabel set off in pursuit of Mortimer who, not interested in parables, had wandered off.

"Keep an eye on my Billy, will you, dear," called one mother. "That's him along by the gate with his wheely dog—"

At the Town Hall, Mrs Jones had decorated the Mayor's office with streamers, balloons, and paper tablecloths over the desks.

Mr Bonnybuy tapped at the door and came in.

"Say! This looks like *fun!*" he exclaimed. "Er – I don't believe I've had the pleasure—?" He held out his hand to Mrs Jones, who beamed.

"Bonnybuy, BB to you!"

"You can call me Mrs Jones. I'm his Honour's temporary asset."

"Looks like you're getting fixed up for a party? Why don't I give you a hand?" offered Mr BB.

"Well, I won't say no!" said Mrs Jones.

By the time the Mayor and Barnoff came back, Mrs Jones and Mr Bonnybuy were getting on splendidly, drinking milkshakes and eating popcorn.

"Good heavens, Mr Bonnybuy! We hadn't expected you quite so early. But I'm glad to see Mrs Jones has been entertaining you."

"She's been telling me tales of Old Rumbury," said

Mr BB. "The Devil's Fault, or is it the Rumbury Ballroom?"

"Oh, just a lot of old tales." The Mayor laughed nervously.

"I'd sure like to take a look at that Ballroom. But not this trip," said Mr BB. "Now – you want to sell me that building?" He pointed to a picture of Tower Heights on the wall. "Well – it's an old heap, it's full of bats, and it's built on a fault – but it suits me fine; I'll *buy* it!"

The Mayor was so relieved that he spilled popcorn all over the floor.

"What will you do with it, Mr BB?"

"That's my little secret, Mr Mayor!"

"Oh, by the way, Mr Cutlink," said Mrs Jones, "I've a message for you from Professor Tigran. He wants to augment his Gift Ceremony at the full moon, four days from now."

"Is this another of your old Rumbury Rites?" asked Mr BB, all agog.

"We have a Statue Unveiling Ceremony," the Mayor explained. "It is a gift in return for overseas aid."

"Great!" cried Mr Bonny. "I'm planning a little ceremony myself; why don't we combine?"

"I was going to suggest that myself," said the Mayor. "We planned to site the statue by the Tower Heights and open the ceremony with a Song Contest."

"*I love it!*" shouted Mr BB. "Let me be your sponsor! I'll give a year's supply of chocolate bars to the lucky winner of the contest."

And he whipped out a huge cheque-book.

In the park Professor Tigran was saying: "Now ghere ze moral of ze story I told you is clear..."

The mums were all sitting in a row, looking at him very peacefully. But Arabel, looking anxious, said to one of them: "Please, I'm afraid I can't go on looking after your Billy any longer. My raven has gone off. I think he may have gone home; I have to go after him . . ."

Back at Number Six, Rainwater Crescent, Mortimer had piled up a whole heap of objects, chairs, buckets, boxes, and saucepans in order to reach the Professor's gong-stick, which had been left well out of reach (or so the Professor thought) on top of the grandfather clock. At last Mortimer managed to knock down the gong-stick on to the floor. It fell with a loud crash, but this did not wake Mr Jones who was still sitting, wrapped in slumber, at the kitchen table. (Professor Tigran had put him into a sleep so deep that he did not wake until bed-time, when he simply went to bed and slept some more.)

Mortimer dragged the stick through his raven-flap.

He did pause thoughtfully, for a minute, beside the huge hole in Mr Leggit's garden. Should he drop the stick in there? But no, in the end he decided not to.

In the street, dragging the stick, he met Mrs Jones, hurrying homewards.

"Mortimer!" she gasped. "What ever have you got there? *Mortimer!*"

But he took no notice, and she was too full of interesting news to stop.

"Ben! Ben! Just listen to this!"

But Ben did not answer.

Mortimer went on towards the park, hauling the gong-stick.

"Szo, ladies, you see," the Professor was finishing, "zere is no danger from ze statue – no danger at all . . ."

Suddenly he saw Mortimer approaching the wrapped-up statue, wielding the gong-stick.

The Professor froze with horror.

"No!" he cried. "No, no, not now! *Sztop zat bird!*"

9

Next day, Have-a-Go Flo strolled into the Mayor's office. She carried a copy of the *Rumbury Gazette* and read aloud the headline from it: "TEXAN MILLIONAIRE BUYS RUMBURY'S TOPPLING TOWER. Does this mean I get my six weeks' back wages, your Worship?"

"Ah, yes, yes, of course, of course, as soon as I've cashed the cheque," said Mr Cutlink, hurriedly. "A penny saved is worth a pound of butter."

"You *owe* me a favour or two," said Have-a-Go Flo. "That barmy bird of the Joneses was all set to smash the Gift Statue with a sledgehammer – can you believe it? Lucky I was driving past in the digger – had to grab the bird with the scoop, judged it to a millimetre, beautiful it was – and chuck him over the fence, otherwise your statue would have been sawdust!"

"Let alone the raven," said the Mayor faintly, looking as if he thought this might have been all for the best.

"Oh, *he* was all right," said Flo. "He seems to enjoy a bit of pandemonium."

In the Jones kitchen Mrs Jones was saying, "Ben? Are you all right today? Ben?"

Mr Jones looked up from the paper. "Never better," he said. "Why?"

"Well, you weren't yourself *at all* yesterday! Didn't speak, wouldn't answer! Ever so strange, you was! I thought you were having a cataclysmic seizure!"

"I had a wonderful nap," said Mr Jones. "Until the Professor came in and disturbed me. He's a nice chap – but he will interfere. Today I feel as fresh as a daisy. I see the Mayor managed to sell the Tower Heights. Now, perhaps, they can fix our street."

Five minutes later, Mortimer shot out of his raven-flap trailing bits of gold net, straw, and satin ribbon. Mrs Jones opened the front door and came after him in a fury.

"Mortimer! My best hat! I'll *nevermore* you, when I get hold of you!"

Arabel hurried after her mother.

"Ma! Perhaps you could borrow a hat from Chris's mum – she has a hat library?"

"Go to my own daughter's speech in borrowed plumes? Over my dead body!" said Mrs Jones.

"Mortimer didn't *mean* any harm," said Arabel. "He was hibernating after his upset with the statue."

"One way and another he's trailed the name of Jones in the mud," sniffed her mother.

The Professor came out into the garden.

"Be at peace," he said. "Mrs Jones, all wvill be for the best. In my country a raven under the roof is the sign of grrreat good luck."

"With him under it, he's lucky we've *got* a roof," snapped Mrs Jones, and started for the Town Hall.

Bill and Joe were on their way to Leggit in his tent, bringing him a take-away lunch.

Joe said, "He can't stay here long; the Mayor had a phone call from the prison: they found the Robot going berserk in his cell."

"And we can't keep coming here, we'll be spotted," said Bill.

Have-a-Go Flo swung towards them, whistling.

"Hi, boys! Going up to the park? You can give me a hand with something!"

Shrugging helplessly, they turned and followed her up to the park where they moved the Gift Statue, on a trolley, towards its new site near Rumbury Tower Heights.

Not very far away, Barnoff was saying to Mr Bonnybuy: "We can provide a couple of decorators for you, Mr Bonny, and I hope we can somehow arrange to have the bats shifted."

"Oh, the bats are *fun*, let's keep 'em," said Mr BB, blithely.

He dropped the wrapper of the Mortimer bar he was eating into a nearby litter bin.

Mortimer, who was also nearby on his way to the park with Chris and Arabel, looked with great interest at the wrapper, then worked his way along a bench until he was beside Mr BB. He slipped his beak into Mr BB's trouser pocket, felt around, and fetched out another Mortimer bar. Then he swallowed it.

Arabel came running up with Chris.

"Oh, *Mortimer*!" she cried, dismayed.

"Eh – what's that?" said Mr BB, looking down.

"That's Mortimer," explained Arabel. "He's our raven; he lives with us."

"Can he *talk*?" asked Mr BB.

"Nevermore!" said Mortimer.

"Wow!" Mr BB was greatly impressed. "What else does he do?"

"You name it, really," sighed Chris.

"I guess he likes Mortimer bars?" said Mr BB, bringing out a whole handful of them.

"Kaaark!" said Mortimer.

Mr Jones, feeling a new man, was washing his taxi in Rainwater Crescent. Then he carefully covered it over with a large, green tarpaulin.

In the Town Hall, Mrs Jones was having hysterics.

"You mean," she screamed at the Mayor, "that evil, idle Mr Leggit has been let loose into the community – about to wreak vengeance on our raven – my Arabel – alone in the park – and no one lifting a finger?"

"Lots of fingers are being lifted, Mrs Jones. In our pie, no stone is unturned. I'll radio Barnoff to look out for your daughter; he's up at the Tower—"

"Up at the Tower! He'll have her encapsulated on the fortieth floor!"

Professor Tigran met Have-a-Go Flo in the Jones garden.

"Oh, hello Professor," she said. "Are you coming up to the Tower to see your statue settled in?"

"Ghyes, ghyes, I am just rrready. You are writing a book?" he asked, noticing a bundle of printed papers under her arm.

"No, no," said Flo, "this is just the instructions for an underground video camera. The Mayor wants me to check out this hole under the street – see what's down there."

"Ah ha," said the Professor. "Zis could be most interesting. I, too, ghwould like to see wvat is down zere."

Leggit, listening to them in his tent, said to the

pigeon: "Did you hear that, Pio Nono? It's time for us to move house. And where are Bill and Joe with my breakfast?"

He peered out at the sign which Chris had stuck up.

"MORTIMER'S MINE, hah! If he *was* I'd know what to do with him!"

Up in the park, Arabel, Chris, and Seleena were having a wonderful time practising songs. Mortimer was not having such a wonderful time. He had eaten twenty-seven Mortimer bars, given him by Mr BB, and was lying on his side, heaving feebly.

Chris sang:

"When your heart's in the dumps and your brain's in decline
When you're bored and ignored, and no one's got time
Then there's only one thing that can make it all fine
And Mortimer's, Mortimer's, Mortimer's mine!
You could offer me buckets of diamonds that shine
Or say that I'll be the whole world's Valentine
I know what I'd choose, I'd refuse every time
'Cos Mortimer's, Mortimer's, Mortimer's mine."

"What makes a shiver run right down your spine?" sang Seleena.

"What will the answer be, time after time?" sang Arabel.

94

"What will you find at the end of the line?" sang Chris.

"Mortimer's mine! No, mine! No, mine!" they all sang together. *"Mortimer's, Mortimer's, Mortimer's mine!"*

Bill and Joe were puzzled. They had hurried back from the park to Rainwater Crescent, carrying Mr Leggit's take-away, which by now had gone cold. But Leggit was not in the tent.

"Maybe the cops got him?" suggested Joe. "Sent dogs down the tunnel?"

"Please!" begged Bill. "Not on an empty stomach!"

"Well, we did our best. We can't get involved any more."

"Let's go and see the man about the job."

Off they went to the Town Hall, singing and dancing.

Mrs Jones met the Professor in Rainwater Crescent. She was in floods of tears.

"I got home from work and found my Arabel's missing!" she wailed. "And Mortimer too, for the matter of that."

"Please, do not wvorry so," urged the Professor. "W̄ve wvake Mr Jones and perghaps ghe can ghunt for them in taxi."

"That maniac's got a grudge against our Mortimer," wept Mrs Jones, "*goodness* knows why, he's just a harmless, brainless bird – and my Arabel's only little—"

They went into the house.

Two minutes later Arabel, Chris, and Mortimer came along the street. Chris carried Mortimer, who was still feeling extremely unwell. As they passed Mr Jones's taxi, Arabel said, "Do you think I should tell Ma that Mr Bonny offered us ten thousand dollars for Mortimer?"

"What good would that do?" said Chris. "You said no."

"Well, we'd better not tell her, then. Come on, Mortimer. Time for tea!"

Mortimer let out a deathly gasp. "*Nevermore . . .*"

They went into the house.

Inside the tarpaulin-covered taxi, Leggit whispered to his pigeon: "Hey, Pio Nono! This is my lucky day! A Texan millionaire with ten thousand dollars going spare – and he wants that stupid bird! Come on, Pio! This is your moment of glory, you can do it for old Legs. *Bring me back the raven!*"

"Ooooh! hoo!" said the pigeon, aghast.

10

Next morning, up at Rumbury Tower Heights, Bill and Joe were surveying the Gift Statue resting on its trolley in front of the tower building.

"Rummy sort of gift, if you ask me," said Joe.

"Looks to me," said Bill, "as if it's shrunk a bit since we fetched it up here."

"P'raps it's homesick," suggested Joe. "This place is pretty bleak."

"Well, *we've* got to brighten things up," said Bill.

They had pots of paint, spray cans, and brushes.

"Yes, and look where that's getting us – up the perishing tower! I don't like heights!"

"Cheer up," said Bill, "makes a change from going down the mine. Come on, we'd better cover up that thing. Don't want to spill paint on it."

They draped a large green tarpaulin over the statue.

At the Jones house, Arabel was in the lounge practising her speech. Dust sheets had been draped over all the furniture because of the dust that came out of the huge crack in the wall.

"That's very good, lovey," said Mrs Jones, who had

been listening to Arabel. "*I* could *never* learn all those long words."

Seleena was there too. "Does this look right, Professor?" she asked, draping a Greek robe over Arabel.

"I don't think I can walk with it like that," said Arabel.

"No matter. You wvill stand, by ze statue," the Professor told her. "Wvearring green leaves in ze ghair, you will be tree nymph, dryad, symbol of future growth."

Mortimer hopefully wound himself up in a curtain too.

"What will Mortimer do?" asked Arabel.

"Aftair your speech he wvill strike ze you-know-what; vun, tvoo, zree – yes?"

"But what will he wear?"

"*I'm* the one that needs a costume!" snapped Mrs Jones. "After he ate my hat."

"Why don't you pop next door and have a look at what Mrs Cross has to offer?" suggested her husband.

"Well – maybe I will – just for a minute . . ." said his wife.

When Mrs Jones stepped out from the house in Rainwater Crescent, a large van was pulling up behind her husband's taxi. On its side were written the words CANDY IS DANDY. Mr Bonnybuy jumped out of the van, walked past Have-a-Go Flo, who was drilling near Mr Leggit's garden with a huge drill, and approached Mrs Jones.

"Mrs Jones!" he shouted. "Mrs Jones! Can I have a word?"

Inside Mr Jones's taxi, under the tarpaulin, Mr Leggit softly rolled down the window and listened with all his ears.

He heard Mrs Jones say, "My Arabel was only acting according to her upbringing, Mr Beddy Byes! If a strange man offered *me* ten thousand dollars for a bird in the hand, *I'd* have my suspicions."

"But if you'd sell him to me," said Mr Bonnybuy, "he'd live a life of luxury, and so would you!"

"Sell our Mortimer?" cried Mrs Jones. "Break our Arabel's heart? I'd sooner be nibbled to death by ducks! You can change the name of your chocolate bar, Mr Thing. Mortimer bar, indeed! Intoxicating a poor slaven into ravery – I mean raven into slavery—"

Mrs Jones rushed away from Mr BB towards Mrs Cross's house.

"Only trying to help, Mrs J!" he called after her.

"I tell you, Mr Bon Bon, the answer is *No!*"

Shrugging, Mr Bonnybuy returned to his van.

Mr Leggit popped his head out of the taxi window, from under the tarpaulin.

"Mr Bonny! Hey! Mr Bonny! Pssst! Wait! About the bird! – Oh, curses!"

For Mr Bonnybuy had not heard him over the noise of Flo's drilling, and was going back to his van.

"Quick!" said Leggit, shoving Pio Nono out of the taxi. "Get in there, stop him!"

Mortimer, in the Jones front room, happened to look out of the window. A vengeful light came into his eye. Ignoring the fact that Arabel and Seleena had draped him in a piece of sheet, he flopped to the floor, causing a lot of pins to fall with him, and shot out through his raven-flap.

A moment later Mr Jones, also looking out of the window, shouted: *"Hey!* What the dickens! *My taxi!* If Mortimer's in there, I'll boil him in oil!"

For the taxi – tarpaulin and all – had started up and was following a van along Rainwater Crescent.

Mr Jones rushed out. "Who the blazes half-inched my taxi?" he asked Have-a-Go Flo. She stopped drilling.

"Well, I'm blessed!" she said, looking round. "It was there just now. And nobody near! This place is really spooky!"

Bill and Joe, with paintbrushes and spray cans, were hanging in a basket halfway up the side of Rumbury Tower Heights.

Bill was saying: "I can't look. I can't bear it. I feel sick! I want to go home . . ."

Joe said, "Oh, do pull yourself together! Bonny's the richest man in Texas – we can't let him down."

"Don't say that!"

"Keep quiet – or you'll start a bat panic. Remember, they warned us, no loud noises up here."

"A b-b-b-bat panic? B-b-b-b-bother the b-b-b-bats!" moaned Bill, hanging on to the side of the basket.

In Rainwater Crescent the Professor was saying, "I wvill come wviz you, Mr Jones. I wvould like to ghelp."

"All right," said Mr Jones. "Arabel, you wait here for your Ma. And you too, Miss Seleena, if you'll be so kind."

"Of course, you must go, quickly, after your taxi," said Seleena.

"But where's Mortimer?" said Arabel.

"I've my own suspicions," said Mr Jones grimly. "I left the keys in the ignition. If that blessed bird—"

Arabel turned very pale. "Oh, *no*, Pa! He *wouldn't*—"

By now, Mr Bonnybuy's van had pulled up at the side of Rumbury Tower Heights. Mr BB jumped out and looked up to see how the work was going. Quietly, the taxi pulled up behind the van. Mr Leggit stealthily slipped out of the taxi and crept along to Mr BB.

In a low voice he said: "Mr Bonny? You don't know me. But I know what you're after. You want to buy the raven, yes?"

"Say," said Mr BB, "news travels fast round here. Who are *you*?"

"I can get that bird for you!" hissed Mr Leggit. "Ten thousand dollars and he's yours!"

"Is that so?"

"He's here now!" whispered Leggit. "I lured him into your van. Come and see!"

They went round the van and opened the doors at the back. Out tumbled an avalanche of boxes, Mortimer bars, and wrappings. Also Pio Nono, with a Mortimer bar jammed over his beak.

"Hey!" said Mr Bonny, laughing. "He's cute, but he's not the one I'm after. Sorry!"

And he walked away.

Leggit turned furiously on the pigeon. "You idiot! Where's Mortimer? How did he get away?"

"Ooroo," said the pigeon, miserably, through the Mortimer bar.

The basket containing Bill and Joe was descending slowly on its rope, while another basket, containing bricks, paint, and building materials, travelled slowly upwards. This basket also contained Mortimer, who, looking all around, was thoroughly enjoying himself.

"Nevermore," he muttered happily, looking at the huge view.

On the other side of Tower Heights, Mr Jones and the Professor came rushing up to the tarpaulin-covered statue on its trolley. They pulled off the covers.

"But *that's* not my taxi!" said Mr Jones, bitterly disappointed.

"*Oimoi!* But ghwhat ghas ghappened?" demanded the Professor, staring at the statue. "Ghit ghas changed! Ze statue ghas changed! Now ghwhy, I ask myself?"

Mr Jones paid little attention to this.

"We'd better go home," he muttered. "If I can't find the taxi – or Mortimer – Arabel will be worried stiff—"

"Very well. We go ghome," said the Professor, deep in thought. He scraped off a little of the statue's surface, some black, some white, and wrapped it in his handkerchief.

Bill and Joe climbed out of their basket. Bill was weak and trembling and the colour of well-mixed mustard.

"Hey," said Mr Bonnybuy, "you don't look so hot, fella – come on, I'll buy you lunch."

"That'd be great!" said Joe. "I could eat a horse. How about you, Bill?"

"Ooooh!" moaned Bill.

As they walked away, Leggit crept from behind a pillar.

"Don't say those oafs are working for *him*, now?" he muttered. "Where's their loyalty? What about me?"

"Boo hoo," said the pigeon.

A long way above them, Mortimer, whose basket was now right up at the top of the tower, was clambering on to a window sill and looking through to see what was inside.

"The raven must be up there," muttered Leggit, staring skywards. "Go on—" to the pigeon, "– why don't you fly up there and chase him down? Oh, all right—" as the pigeon flinched, "– *I'll* do it – here—"

And, seizing the pigeon's whistle, Mr Leggit blew a long piercing blast on it.

Up above, Mortimer, much surprised by the noise, fell backwards into the basket, which began whizzing down again.

In Rainwater Crescent, Mr Jones was saying to Arabel: "Now, let me get this straight. The Texas tycoon wanted to buy Mortimer? Well of course he can't, Mortimer's his own bird. It's my taxi I'm worried about. Who would have taken it? And where can they have put it? Everyone knows it round here – unless Mortimer took it? Is Martha still next door trying on hats? Maybe I'll step round and fetch her."

In fact, Mrs Jones was just returning with a huge stack of hats in her arms. Behind her, racing in terror, came Mr Leggit, pursued by a cloud of bats, and with a terrified pigeon flapping over his head.

The bats, reaching Mrs Jones, swarmed round her.

"Help!" she shouted. "What's happening?"

"Oh – *no!*" yelled Leggit, seeing Mrs Jones, and he made a dive for the hole in his garden.

"It's that Monster! It's him!" cried Mrs Jones in horror, and she collapsed on to a pile of hats.

"Martha! Speak to me!" cried Mr Jones, finding her in a heap, and he slapped her face and hands.

Seleena, Arabel, and the Professor came running out of the house.

"Oh, Ben!" whispered Mrs Jones. "I *saw* him! Right here!"

"Who?"

"I saw him. With my very own eyes. He went – down there—"

Mrs Jones pointed shakily to the hole.

"*There's* Mortimer!" cried Arabel joyfully.

For Mortimer came crashing through the hedge from Leggit's garden, with swarms of bats all around him.

"Nevermore!" he shouted proudly.

"Eureka!" cried the Professor. "Now I ghave it! Zis is incredible!"

"Have what?" said Mr Jones, impatiently. "Come on, Martha – up you get!"

"All is revealed!" exulted the Professor, dancing on the path.

"Professor, please – there is no need for you to go crazy," urged Seleena.

"No – no – not crazy – *bats!*" cried the happy Professor.

11

Next day, a police constable came to Number Six, Rainwater Crescent to inquire about the theft of Mr Jones's taxi.

"And you'd better catch that escaped prisoner while you're at it!" said Mrs Jones, sharply. "All the time you've been dillying and dallying he could have climbed out of that hole and eloped."

"Oh, I don't think so, Mrs Jones," said the constable. "We've got the hole under surveillance."

Meanwhile the Professor, with jars of chemicals, was working on his samples of the statue, trying to discover what had made it shrink. He was dropping bits of stone into little jars of liquid.

Out in the garden, Have-a-Go Flo was lowering long pipes into the hole. Huge boxes full of cables and TV equipment stood about. Mr Barnoff from the Town Hall was there with a clipboard.

"Good morning, Mr Jones," he said, when Mr Jones stepped outside. "I'm just compiling a list of items that are missing in the town – have you anything to add to it?"

"A black taxi," said Mr Jones, gloomily.

"Do you suspect that it is down the hole?"

"Everything *else* seems to be," said Mr Jones.

"My best tablecloth," said Mrs Jones, coming out; "our stair carpet, the stair rods, not to mention all those antique cactuses from the Town Hall. Rumbury Council ought to pay for this, Mr Bareface! If this hole had been filled in from the word go, none of all that's happened would have happened – let alone escaped marauders hiding down there. I'll bring the whole town down on your heads if action is not taken!"

"Have we offered a reward for recapturing the escaped prisoner?" the constable whispered to Barnoff, who whispered back, "Perhaps Mr Bonnybuy would hand out a year's supply of chocolate bars . . ."

Bill and Joe, who had worked all night, were yawning at the foot of Rumbury Tower Heights.

Bill said, "Next time, I'd rather go to prison. This caring for the community is a killer."

"Cheer up," said Joe. "One more day of it, and we're free as air. Maybe Mr B will invite us to Texas. I feel sorry for old Leggit, stuck down that mine. And if they do get him out, they'll only send him back to prison."

"Oh, look," said Bill, noticing the taxi, still covered with its tarpaulin. "We'd better shove that thing out of sight. It's only an old motor someone must have dumped here. Let's push it under the tower, out of harm's way."

They did so.

In Rainwater Crescent, the mums of Rumbury were parading with a new set of placards. SAVE THE BATS and BATS MUST GO FREE said their signs.

"Good morning, ladies," said Seleena, coming with Chris to drop in at the Jones house. "I see you have a new cause – Help the Bats?"

"Those bats have lived in Rumbury for hundreds of years," shouted a mum. "They have their rights, same as humans."

"They've been kidnapped – batnapped – shut underground – it's downright cruel!" shouted another mum.

Barnoff, in the Jones garden, was talking to the Mayor on his portable phone.

"You'll have to look after the school party at Rumbury Heights, sir. Better put on your Mayoral costume, that would go down big with the kids."

The phone snarled at him furiously.

In the Jones kitchen, Mr Jones was saying, "That bird has got to stay in the house all day today! Yesterday he caused too much trouble. He's got to learn. Do you hear, Mortimer?"

Furiously, Mortimer jumped into the sink, which was full of water and dishes.

"He's taking a nice warm bath," said Arabel.

To Mortimer she added, consolingly, "We'll practise your song today, Mortimer, so it'll be really good for the festival tomorrow."

"Nevermore!" muttered Mortimer.

That afternoon, up at Rumbury Tower Heights, in front of the statue on its trolley still covered by green tarpaulin, the Mayor was getting ready to address an army of school-children. He wore his scarlet robes and great feathered hat. He carried a large sack of acorns. Behind him was a poster which said GROW A GREENER RUMBURY.

"Morning, Mr Mayor!" said Mr Bonnybuy, coming round a corner of the building. "What's all this then? Another of your quaint old English customs?"

"A party of Rumbury school-children are coming to plant acorns on Rumbury Waste," the Mayor told him with dignity. "We are restoring an Iron Age forest."

"My!" said Mr BB, much impressed.

The Mayor asked him, "Is the Tower ready for the ceremony tomorrow?"

"Yes, sir! Those boys must have worked all night."

"Then they can clean up the statue," said the Mayor. "It's looking rather queer."

A huge crowd of children arrived from buses. They rushed up to the Mayor.

"Oooh, look! It's Santa Claus! Show us what you've got in that sack!"

"Stop!" shouted the Mayor. But the sack tipped over and a torrent of acorns poured out.

In Rainwater Crescent Barnoff and Have-a-Go Flo were setting up a TV screen, which was connected by pipes and cables to the cave down below.

"I've been having trouble getting a picture," Flo told Barnoff. "There seems to be a huge blockage down there."

Barnoff, studying his clipboard, said, "We have to try and identify some of the items listed here."

"But *they* are probably what's holding up the street," said Flo. "If we take them out – it'll all fall in."

"Oh dear," said Barnoff helplessly. "Any sign of the escaped prisoner?"

"I'm not sure. I must say I'd hate to be down there myself. Come and see."

They both peered at the foggy screen. Slowly, through the murk, a picture formed. There was Leggit, inside a phone box, with cacti packed all around it. Two robots held the door shut. Bats were whirling in front of the box. Leggit's mouth was wide open, and he was rattling the phone box door.

"Do you think he's screaming?" said Flo, nervously.

"No sound," said Barnoff. "Just as well, really," he added.

In the park, Arabel, Chris, and Seleena were practising their song.

"Mortimer's, Mortimer's, Mortimer's mine!" they sang.

"But I just wish Mortimer was *here*," said Arabel, sadly.

"Mortimer will be safer at home," Seleena kindly reassured her.

In the kitchen of the Jones house, Mrs Jones was trying on hats. Mortimer's raven-flap was held shut by a giant hat-pin stuck through the catch. Mortimer was angrily rattling at it, but so far in vain.

"Oh, do give over, Mortimer," said Mrs Jones. "It's for your own good you have to stay in."

Mortimer looked as if he doubted this very much.

"Can't you make yourself useful somehow? What do you think of this hat?"

"Nevermore!" said Mortimer, eyeing the hat with disgust.

"Maybe the green one is more youthful . . ." agreed Mrs Jones.

She tried on another hat. Somebody (goodness knows who) had filled it with salt, which cascaded over her.

"Mercy! What's all this?" she gasped.

Mortimer finally managed to drag out the pin which fastened his raven-flap. As it swung back, a cloud of bats poured through into the room. Blinded, confused, among hats and bats, Mrs Jones staggered to the door and flung it open. More and more bats poured in, and Mortimer shot out.

"Help! I can't see! What's happening?" shouted Mrs Jones.

In the front garden Professor Tigran was dancing about in a cloud of bats, while Mr Jones looked at his garden in horror. Everything – video cables, TV screen, flashing lights and orange tape – was covered in bat droppings.

"Ze bats, ze bats!" cried the Professor, joyfully. "I ghave a premonition, Mr Jones, ghyou know wvat?"

"No, Professor – but I'd believe anything," Mr Jones said, flapping bats away.

"It is the, ghow you say, drippings, that ghaf caused the Negative Poisson Ratio rock from which our island is made!" said the Professor, happily.

"Pollyargos is ghome for many bats! Now I can write a book on zis rock!"

"Sounds like Brighton rock to me," muttered Mr Jones.

Loud screams now came from inside the house and Mortimer shot round the corner, followed by a swarm of bats. He crashed into Flo's TV screen and knocked it into the hole. Mr Jones grabbed hold of Mortimer, and shook him furiously.

Up at Rumbury Tower Heights, Bill and Joe had taken the tarpaulin off the Gift Statue and draped it over the brake-lever of the trolley on which the statue stood. They were scrubbing the statue. As they scrubbed, they sang:

"It's half black and half white
It don't look very good
But we're trying to put it right!
We're working all day
We've been working all night
Sing a song for Rumbury
Until we see the light
And we do –
Wouldn't you?"

Listening to them, Chris, Arabel, and Seleena clapped enthusiastically.

The Professor rushed up, carrying a pile of books and a jam jar full of liquid.

"Look, Professor," said Arabel, "they've been scrubbing the statue for you."

"But ghwhat ghas ghappened?" wailed the Professor, rushing to the statue and fingering its rough surface, half black, half white. "First it shrank – now ghit has grown bigger again! Ze ghwhole process repeats ad infinitum! Ghwho ghwould ghave ghuessed zis? Amazing! I must phone my colleagues immediately!"

He rushed away again, shouting, *"Eureka! Eureka!"*

"Shall we help you put up the speakers' platform?" Seleena asked Bill and Joe.

"Okay! Ta! You're on! We've got the instructions somewhere."

While they were busy putting up the platform, Mortimer appeared looking rumpled and began studying the statue, which had now been covered up again with its green tarpaulin, just like Mr Jones's taxi.

"Kaaark," he murmured thoughtfully. Then he took hold of the trolley brake.

"Hey!" shouted Joe. "Get that bird off there."

"Mortimer!" called Arabel. "Wait – wait – *that's* not Pa's taxi!"

12

Next morning the Jones family, with the Professor and Mortimer and Chris, all dressed in their best, were setting out on foot for Rumbury Heights.

"You are missing your taxi, eh, Mr Jones?" said the Professor sympathetically. "But do not worry, I ghave a premonition."

"I only hope it's better than the last," sighed Mr Jones, who was in his best suit.

Mrs Jones had on a very dashing hat with black and white feathers. Every now and then Mortimer gave it a thoughtful stare. He was being carried by Arabel. The Professor had the gong-stick. He was taking no chances. Chris carried a scroll.

Up at Rumbury Tower Heights the statue, completely uncovered, sat on its trolley. But the Tower building was draped in pink parachute nylon. TV cameras stood all round.

Mr Bonnybuy was bustling about.

"Okay, boys?" he said to Bill and Joe. "Are you all set with the cameras?"

"Sure thing," said Joe.

"Just say the word," said Bill.

The Mayor arrived, in his robes.

"Morning, your Worship!" cried Mr BB. "Will you say a few words?"

"I was going to ask if you'd like to judge our Song Contest," said Mr Cutlink. "Since you are so kindly providing the prize."

"Great! Great!" Mr BB dashed away again. The Mayor looked after him nervously.

"I always get the feeling that he's laughing at me," he said to Barnoff.

"If we can only get through today, it'll be all over," Barnoff consoled him.

"What a programme!" sighed the Mayor. "A dangerous statue, unpopular with mums; a leaning tower; and, to cap it all, I have to listen to the Rumbury Rap. Ah, here's the Professor."

"Good morning, Mr Cutlink. I ghave found out a ghreat discovery!"

"That's nice," said the Mayor, faintly. "Finding's keeping, but seeing's believing."

Mrs Jones and Seleena were draping Arabel's costume round her.

"I see they've draped the Tower too," said Mr Jones. "Good thing. Real eyesore that place was."

"Oh, that's just the cover, Pa," Arabel told him. "Soon they're going to take it off."

117

"Kaaark," said Mortimer, picking up his gong-stick and whirling it.

"Not you, my boy, you'll get your turn later," said Mr Jones. "And I only hope the Professor doesn't live to regret it."

Mortimer headed for the Tower in its pink petticoats.

"Oh, dear!" said Arabel. "Chris! Fetch him back, quick!"

Chris dived after Mortimer under the parachute nylon.

Then he shot out again.

"Mr Jones. Mr Jones! Come and see what's here!"

"Ladies and Gentlemen!" announced the Mayor, standing on the platform. "Welcome to the Rumbury Song Contest and Grand Unveiling Ceremony. First, to start the fun, come Bill, Joe, and Flo!"

Having started the cameras running, Bill, Joe, and Flo sang:

"We're half black, and half white
We used to get in trouble
But we've tried to put it right!
Throw out the junk
Fill up the cracks,
First you take it all away
Then you put it back!"

Everybody cheered.

On the other side of the Tower Heights, Mr Jones was gloating over his restored taxi.

"Mortimer, I take back everything I said about you. Martha! Martha! He found my taxi! And the keys are still in it."

"Oh, Mortimer," said Arabel, "you are *clever*."
Mortimer preened himself.

"I just hope he hasn't anything else up his sleeve," said Mrs Jones.

"Come on, Arabel," said Chris. "It's nearly time for you. Put that wreath on."

In front of the Mayor's platform, Chris helped Mortimer (with his gong-stick) on to the trolley where the statue waited.

"Now – stay *still*, Mortimer!" he warned.
Mortimer's eyes sparkled.

"Have you checked the brake on that trolley?" said the Mayor anxiously. "It's downhill all the way from here to Rainwater Crescent."

Meanwhile, in Rainwater Crescent, a constable was just lowering a food parcel in a basket to the imprisoned Mr Leggit.

In the cave, Mr Leggit had at last managed to battle his way out of the phone box. One of the

robots suddenly came to life and began sweeping
feebly about, its light giving off a dim glow. Then it
fell forward on to the food basket.

"Oh, do get out of the way, you stupid thing!"
snapped Leggit. "Much good *you've* been! That
basket is for me. Sandwiches! How kind! Here, Pio,
you'd better climb in the basket and go up. Find that
raven for me. Then I can pay my way out of this
mess."

Sulkily, the pigeon climbed into the basket and
was pulled up to the top, where he flew away, greatly
startling the constable.

Up at the Tower Heights, Seleena was about to sing.

"Just tell me when this one's over, I daren't look,"
said the Mayor, shutting his eyes and clapping his
hands over his ears.

"But, your Worship!" cried Mr BB, "this is where
we unveil the Tower. You can't miss this!"

He passed the Mayor a pair of goggles.

Seleena sang:

"I have lived across the sea
Now I come to Rumbury
Where my heart goes through the ceiling
And I get that golden feeling
NOW . . . !"

The drapes fell away from the tower block,

120

revealing that it was painted all over to look like a mammoth Mortimer bar.

"Ahhhhh!" went the crowd.

"Coo!" said the pigeon, who had just arrived.

Arabel was on the platform to make her speech.

"Deserving citizens of Rumbury, the people of Pollyargos have sent you this piece of their island. They wish you good luck with it. Get well soon!"

"Now," said the Professor to Mortimer. "Vun! Tvoo! Zree!"

"To you too!" said the pigeon rudely to Mortimer.

Turning sharply to protest, Mortimer whacked the trolley-brake with his gong-stick, just missing the pigeon. The trolley started to move, with Mortimer still on it.

"Beware!" shouted the Professor, as Seleena began on the second verse of her song.

"Mortimer Jones! You come back here!" shouted Mrs Jones.

"Wow!" yelled Mr Bonnybuy to Bill and Joe, as Seleena hit her top note. "Just keep filming, you boys!"

With a sound like a million people drinking soup, the tower block sank into the ground. If it had been a person, it would have been up to its knees. Rumbury Waste shook like a jelly; the seesaw in the children's

121

playground bounced up and down; and the swings swung though there was nobody on them.

"To the taxi!" shouted Mr Jones, as the trolley careered away down the hill. "Quick, Martha – Arabel – Professor! We'll take the short cut!"

"Come on, Mr Mayor," said BB, "we'd better keep up with the action."

And he made for his car. Cutlink and Barnoff went with him.

"Let's go!" said Bill to Joe.

Everyone rushed after the escaping statue.

In Rainwater Crescent, the constable sitting by the hole heard a thunderous rumbling coming down the hill towards him. Terrified, he fled in the other direction.

Leggit, just climbing out of the hole, stared in horror as the trolley, with the statue on it and Mortimer waving his club, came bounding towards him down the street.

"Help! Save us!" he wailed, and dived back into the hole again.

Mr Jones arrived from the opposite direction in his taxi just as the trolley hit their garden fence. Although there was a tremendous crash, nobody was hurt. But Mortimer and the statue were flung into the hole after Mr Leggit.

"Stop! Wait! Stand back!" shouted the Professor, leaping from the taxi.

With a huge subterranean boom that made the whole of Rainwater Crescent totter and lurch about, the statue expanded like dough. A manhole in the street flew open, and Leggit shot out of it, clinging to a cactus.

"Get me away from that bird!" he screeched.

The Mayor, stumbling out of BB's car, cried: "Prisoner Leggit, you're under arrest! Barnoff! Grab him!"

"He's all over prickles, sir," said Barnoff, not very willing. But he did grab Leggit.

Mortimer shot out of another manhole, still clutching his gong-stick.

"Mortimer!" said Arabel with delight. "You've filled up your mine!"

"The oracles spoke the truth!" declared the Professor, excitedly. "See the power of the Ghift! Ghit has borne fruit!"

"What else is down there?" asked the Mayor.

"A colony of rare bats!" said the Professor, proudly.

"Not to mention two robots, a load of books, some telephone boxes—" put in Barnoff, studying his clipboard.

"All those antique cactuses and my stair rods," said Mrs Jones.

"And my blood-pressure machine," said Mr Jones.

"Ben Jones!" said Martha, very shocked, "did you put that down there?"

"Don't worry, Martha. I feel a hundred per cent after that ride," said Mr Jones.

"Zose are all offerings to ze statue down zere, vairry good luck," said the Professor.

"Not for the bats, perhaps?" said the Mayor, doubtfully.

"Zey wvill be ghappy down zere," said the Professor. "And ze – ghow you say – droppings wvill make fertilizer – very valuable – and ze rock wvill continue to grow."

"A fertilizer mine, you mean? Fancy!" said Mr Cutlink. "Unusual gift, I must say – but – well – on behalf of Rumbury Town, I think I thank you—"

"It's mine! It's mine!" bawled Leggit, now in handcuffs. "It's on my property!"

"Confiscated for non-payment of debt," said the Mayor. "I say, Barnoff – we can put this fellow on public work therapy now. He can dig it all out!"

Leggit let out a groan.

By now all the crowds from Rumbury Waste had arrived.

"So who won the song contest?" asked Chris.

"I think Miss Seleena hit the bell," said Bonnybuy.

"That stunt with the Tower was really something – better than my wildest dreams."

"And it's still standing," sighed the Mayor, in relief. "An aching leg is better than a broken egg."

"And it will go on standing, as a monument to the bird who made all this possible," said Mr Bonnybuy, handsomely. "And to Miss Seleena, as winner, I am happy to offer a year's supply of Mortimer bars."

"That's *very* kind of you, Mr Bonny," said Seleena. "But I never touch chocolate. Perhaps Mortimer . . ?"

"Kaaark!" said Mortimer.

"I wish I could have bought him," sighed Mr Bonny.

"We could sell you his song?" suggested Chris.

"A Mortimer song? I'd sure like to hear that!" said Mr BB.

So Chris, Arabel, and Seleena sang:

"You could offer me buckets of diamonds that shine,
Or say that I'd be the whole world's Valentine!
I know what I'd choose, I'd refuse every time,
'Cos Mortimer's, Mortimer's, Mortimer's mine!

What makes a shiver run right down your spine?
What will you find at the end of the line?
What will the answer be, time after time?"

Here Mortimer gave the mine sign a terrific whack with his gong-stick. It sank right into the rock, then shot out like a comet as the song ended:

"Mortimer's, Mortimer's, Mortimer's MINE!"

"Eureka!" shouted the Professor.

"Nevermore!" said Mortimer.